ROAD ALLOWANCE ERA

A Girl Called ECHO

VOL. 4

By Katherena Vermette
Illustrated by Scott B. Henderson
Coloured by Donovan Yaciuk

HIGHWATER
PRESS

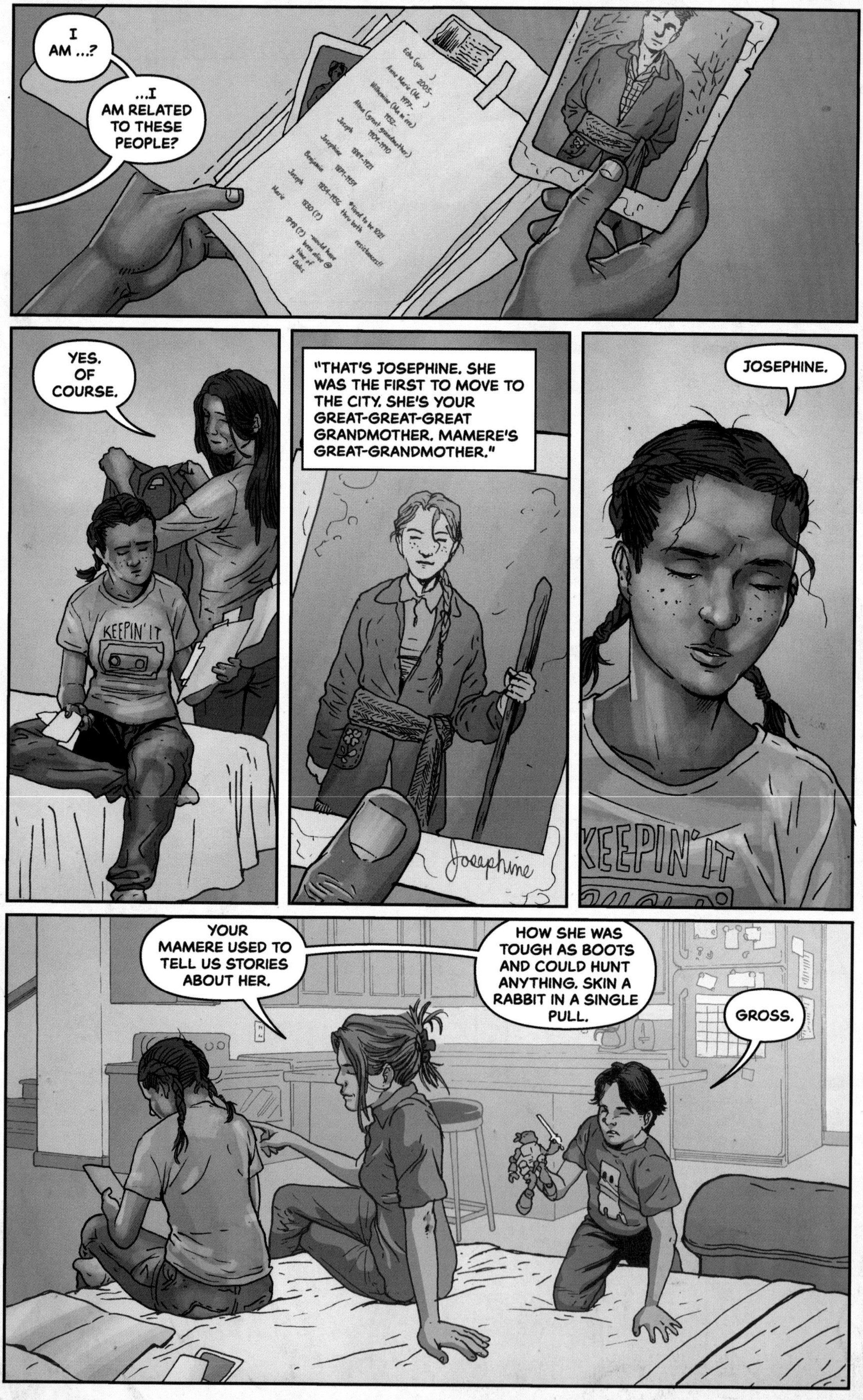
I AM ...?
...I AM RELATED TO THESE PEOPLE?
Echo (you) 2005-
Anne Marie (Me) 1977-
Wilhemine (Mamère) 1952-
Alma (great grandmother) 1909-1990
Joseph 1889-1921
Josephine 1871-1959
Benjamin 1854-1956 *lived to be 102! thru both resistances!!
Joseph 1830 (?)
Marie 1798 (?) -would have been alive @ time of 7 Oaks
YES. OF COURSE.
KEEPIN' IT
"THAT'S JOSEPHINE. SHE WAS THE FIRST TO MOVE TO THE CITY. SHE'S YOUR GREAT-GREAT-GREAT GRANDMOTHER. MAMERE'S GREAT-GRANDMOTHER."
Josephine
JOSEPHINE.
KEEPIN' IT
YOUR MAMERE USED TO TELL US STORIES ABOUT HER.
HOW SHE WAS TOUGH AS BOOTS AND COULD HUNT ANYTHING. SKIN A RABBIT IN A SINGLE PULL.
GROSS.

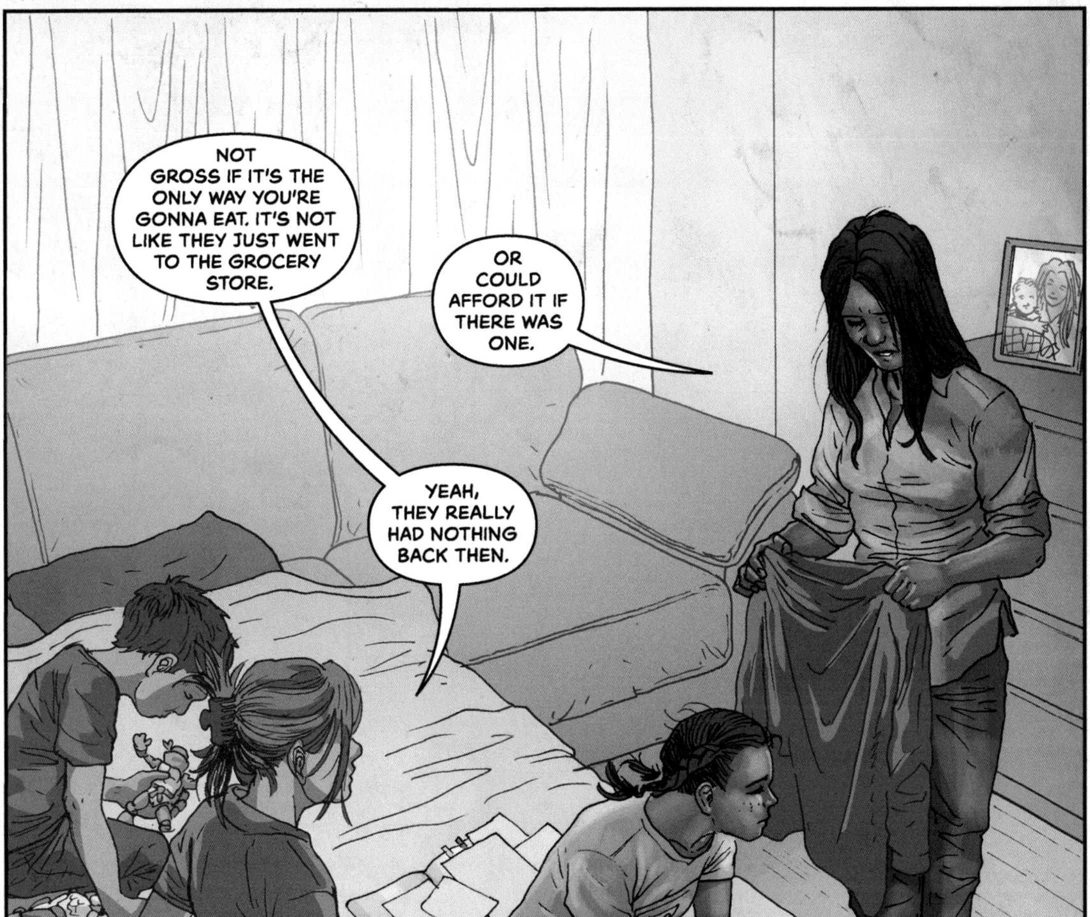
NOT GROSS IF IT'S THE ONLY WAY YOU'RE GONNA EAT. IT'S NOT LIKE THEY JUST WENT TO THE GROCERY STORE.
OR COULD AFFORD IT IF THERE WAS ONE.
YEAH, THEY REALLY HAD NOTHING BACK THEN.

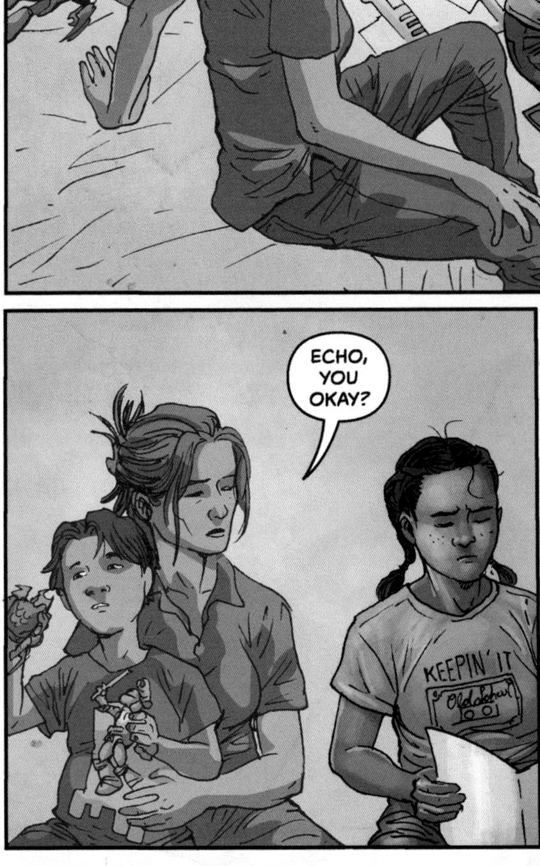
ECHO, YOU OKAY?
KEEPIN' IT

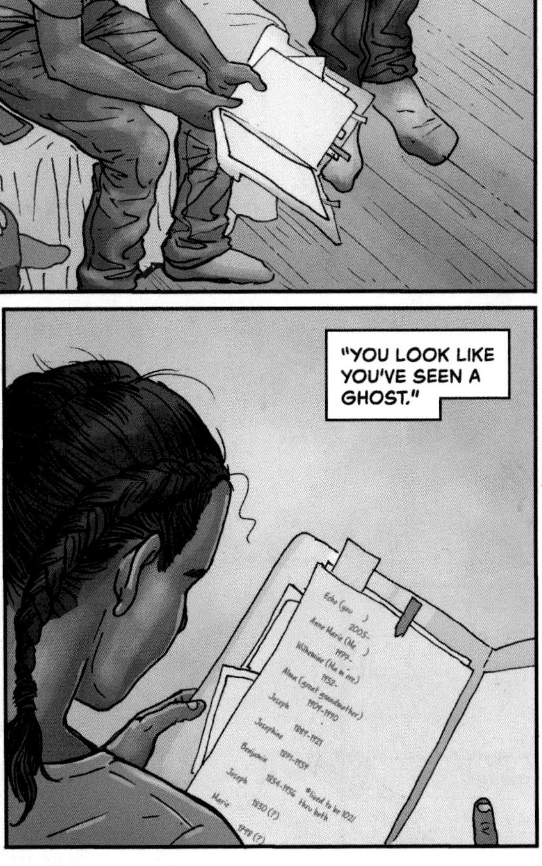
"YOU LOOK LIKE YOU'VE SEEN A GHOST."
Echo (you)
2005-
Anne Marie (Me)
1977-
Wilhemina (Ma m'ere)
1952-
Alma (great grandmother)
Joseph 1909-1990
Josephine 1889-1921
Benjamin 1871-1939
Joseph 1854-1956 *lived to be 102! thru both
Marie 1830 (?)
1798 (?)

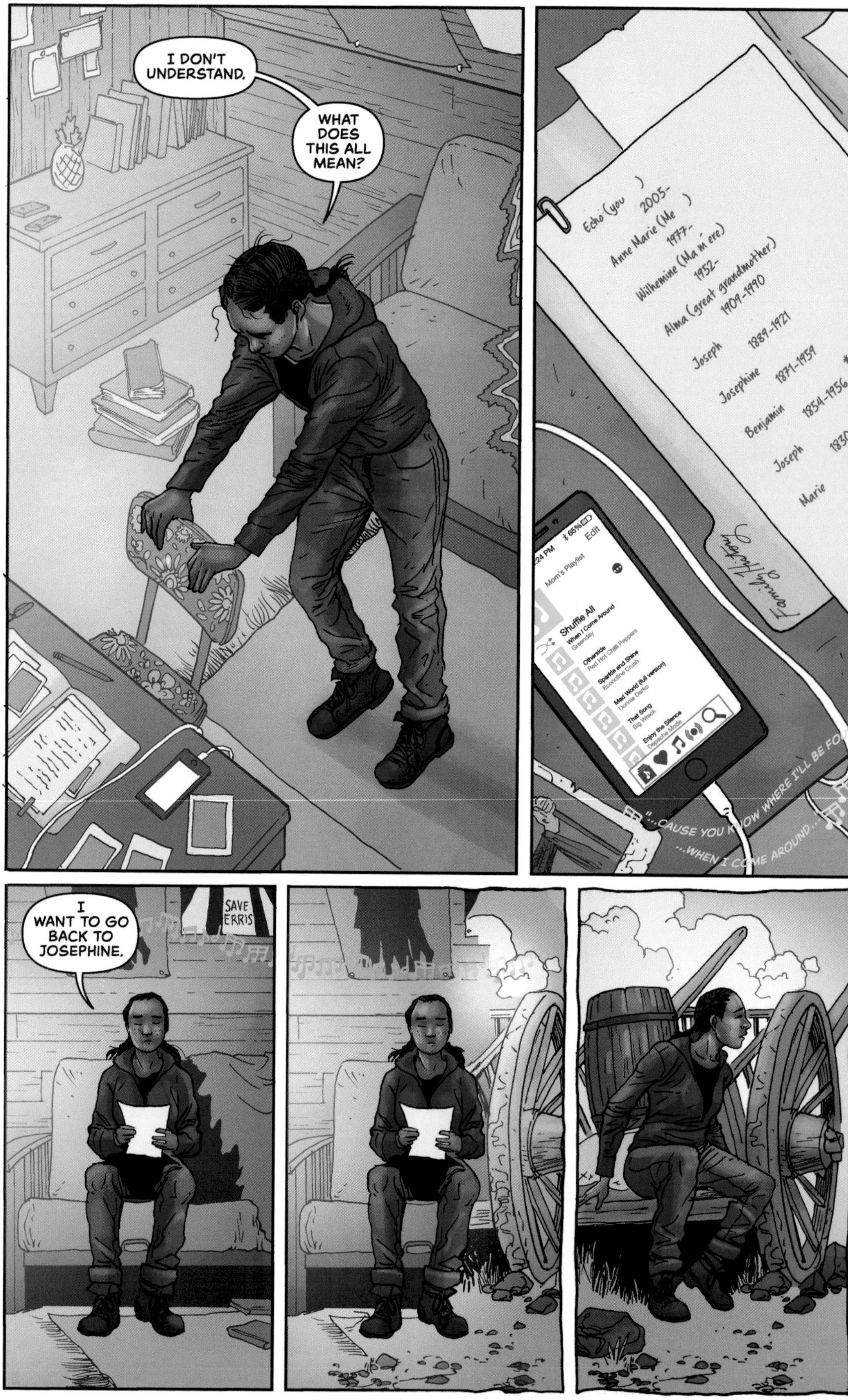
I DON'T UNDERSTAND.
WHAT DOES THIS ALL MEAN?
Echo (you) 2005-
Anne Marie (Me) 1977-
Wilhemine (Ma'm'ere) 1952-
Alma (great grandmother) 1909-1990
Joseph 1889-1921
Josephine 1871-1959
Benjamin 1854-1956
Joseph 1830
Marie
Edit
Mom's Playlist
Shuffle All
When I Come Around
Greenday
Otherside
Red Hot Chili Peppers
Sparkle and Shine
Econoline Crush
Mad World (full version)
Donnie Darko
That Song
Big Wreck
Enjoy the Silence
Depeche Mode
"...CAUSE YOU KNOW WHERE I'LL BE FOU
...WHEN I COME AROUND..."
I WANT TO GO BACK TO JOSEPHINE.
SAVE ERRIS

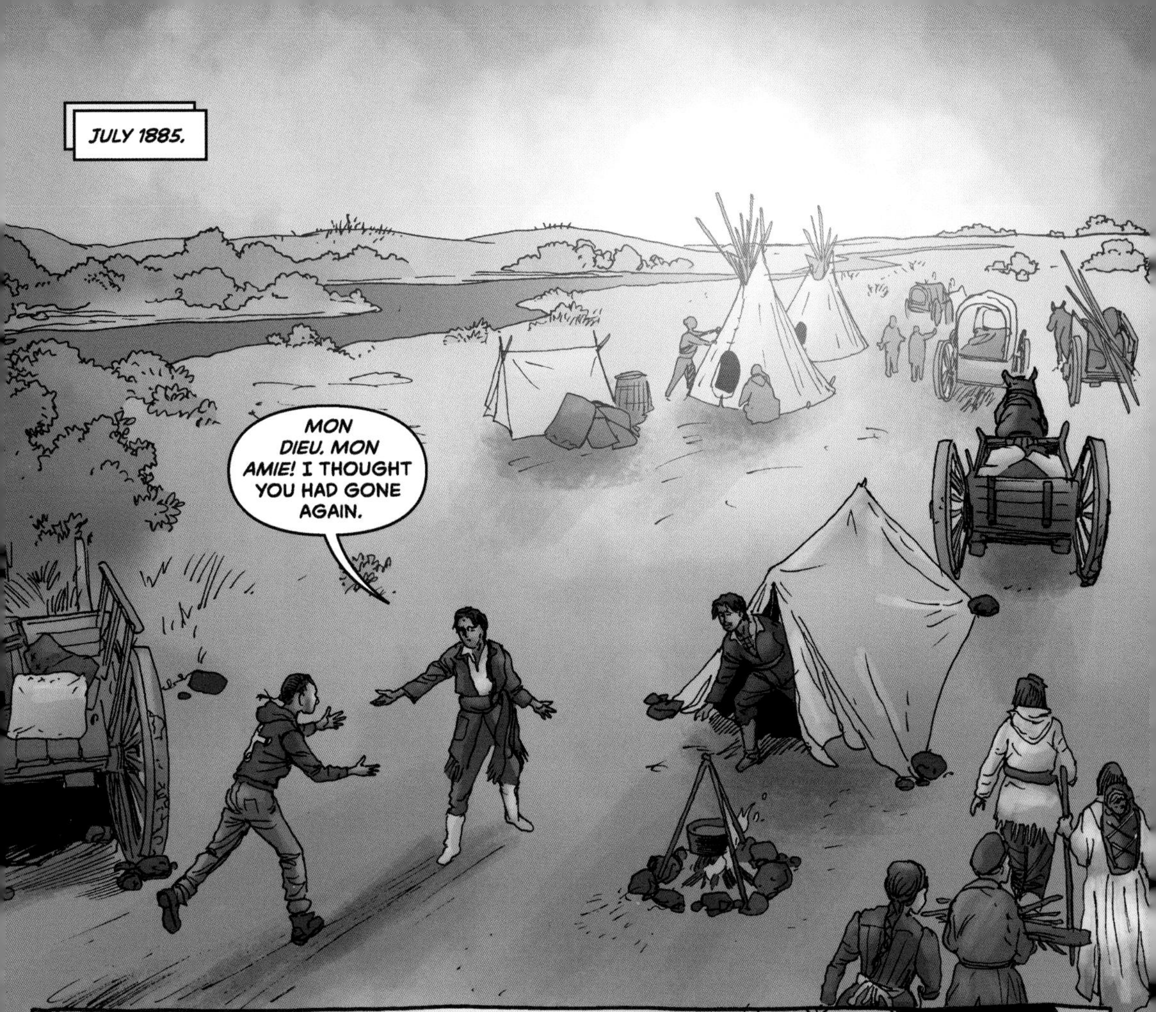
JULY 1885.
MON DIEU. MON AMIE! I THOUGHT YOU HAD GONE AGAIN.

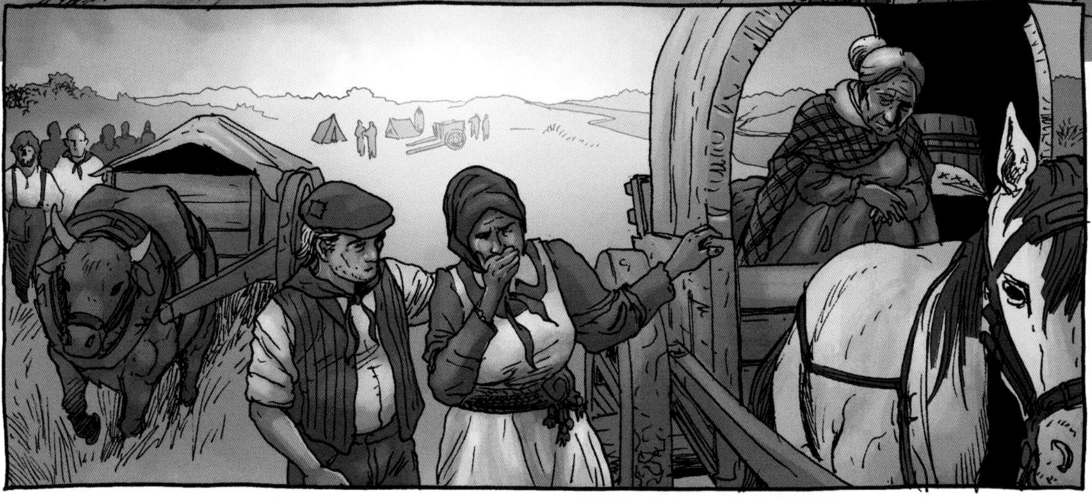

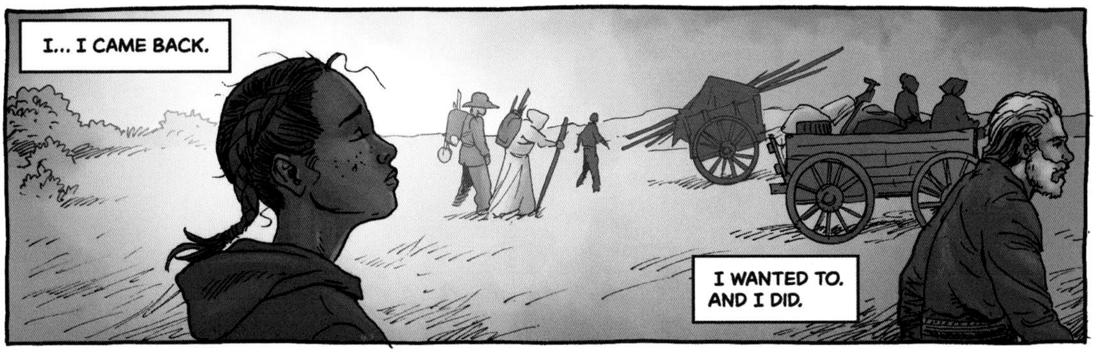
I... I CAME BACK.
I WANTED TO. AND I DID.

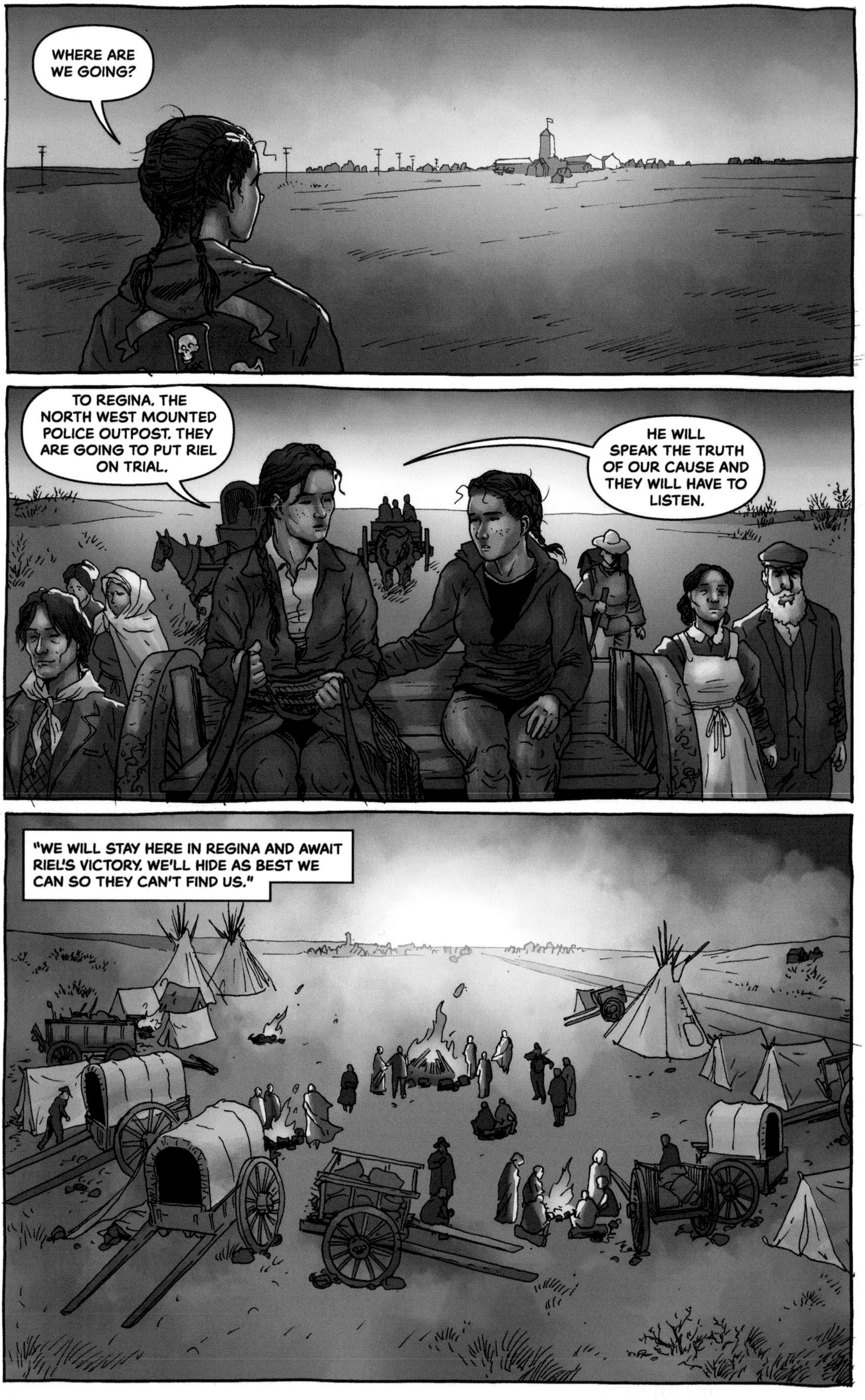
WHERE ARE WE GOING?
TO REGINA, THE NORTH WEST MOUNTED POLICE OUTPOST. THEY ARE GOING TO PUT RIEL ON TRIAL.
HE WILL SPEAK THE TRUTH OF OUR CAUSE AND THEY WILL HAVE TO LISTEN.
"WE WILL STAY HERE IN REGINA AND AWAIT RIEL'S VICTORY. WE'LL HIDE AS BEST WE CAN SO THEY CAN'T FIND US."

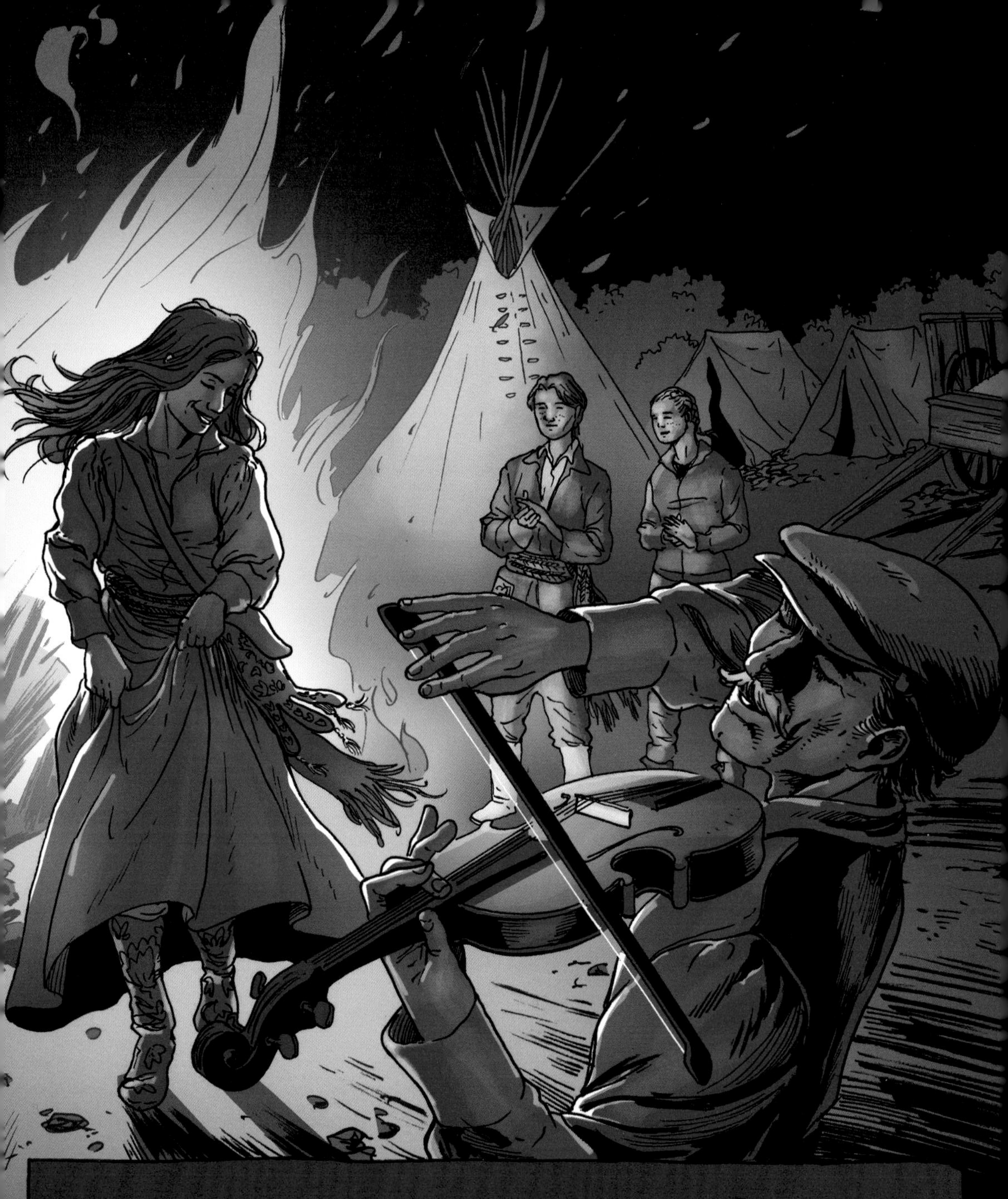

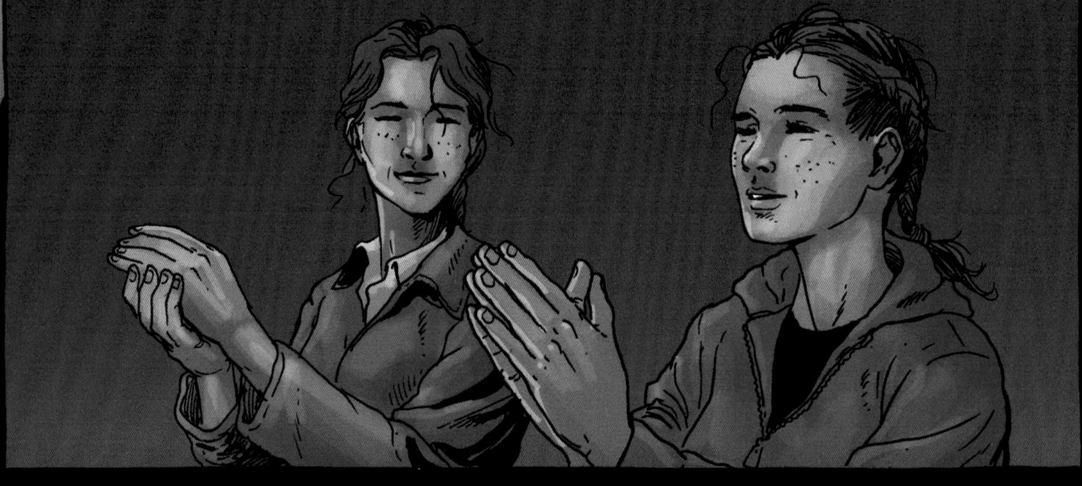

JULY 1885, REGINA COURTHOUSE, THE TRIAL OF LOUIS RIEL.

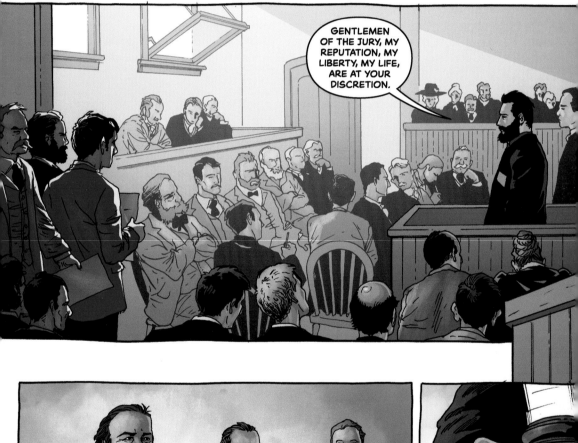

GENTLEMEN OF THE JURY, MY REPUTATION, MY LIBERTY, MY LIFE, ARE AT YOUR DISCRETION.

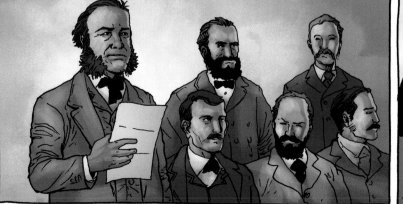

CRACK!

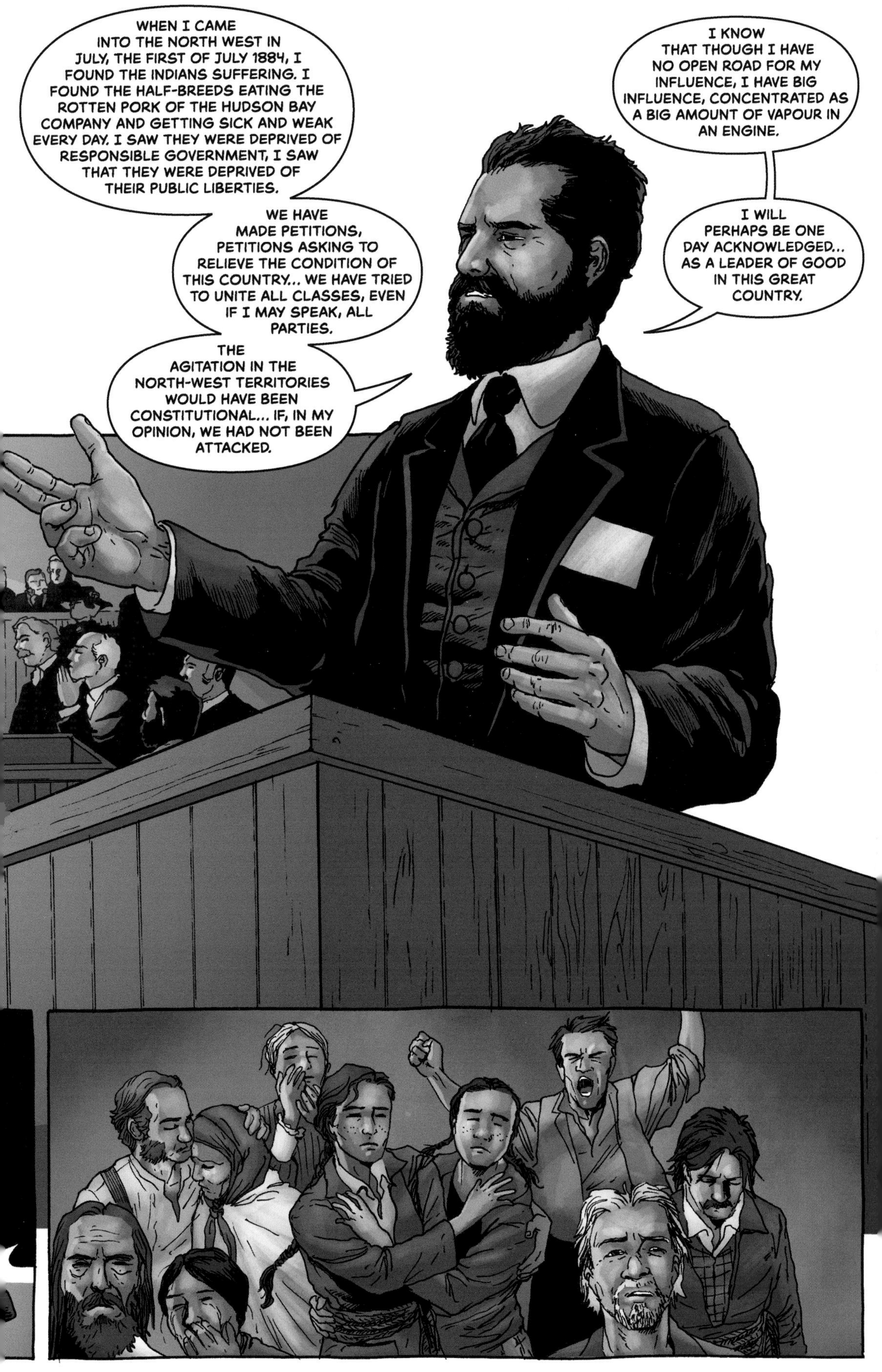
WHEN I CAME INTO THE NORTH WEST IN JULY, THE FIRST OF JULY 1884, I FOUND THE INDIANS SUFFERING. I FOUND THE HALF-BREEDS EATING THE ROTTEN PORK OF THE HUDSON BAY COMPANY AND GETTING SICK AND WEAK EVERY DAY. I SAW THEY WERE DEPRIVED OF RESPONSIBLE GOVERNMENT, I SAW THAT THEY WERE DEPRIVED OF THEIR PUBLIC LIBERTIES.
WE HAVE MADE PETITIONS, PETITIONS ASKING TO RELIEVE THE CONDITION OF THIS COUNTRY... WE HAVE TRIED TO UNITE ALL CLASSES, EVEN IF I MAY SPEAK, ALL PARTIES.
THE AGITATION IN THE NORTH-WEST TERRITORIES WOULD HAVE BEEN CONSTITUTIONAL... IF, IN MY OPINION, WE HAD NOT BEEN ATTACKED.
I KNOW THAT THOUGH I HAVE NO OPEN ROAD FOR MY INFLUENCE, I HAVE BIG INFLUENCE, CONCENTRATED AS A BIG AMOUNT OF VAPOUR IN AN ENGINE.
I WILL PERHAPS BE ONE DAY ACKNOWLEDGED... AS A LEADER OF GOOD IN THIS GREAT COUNTRY.

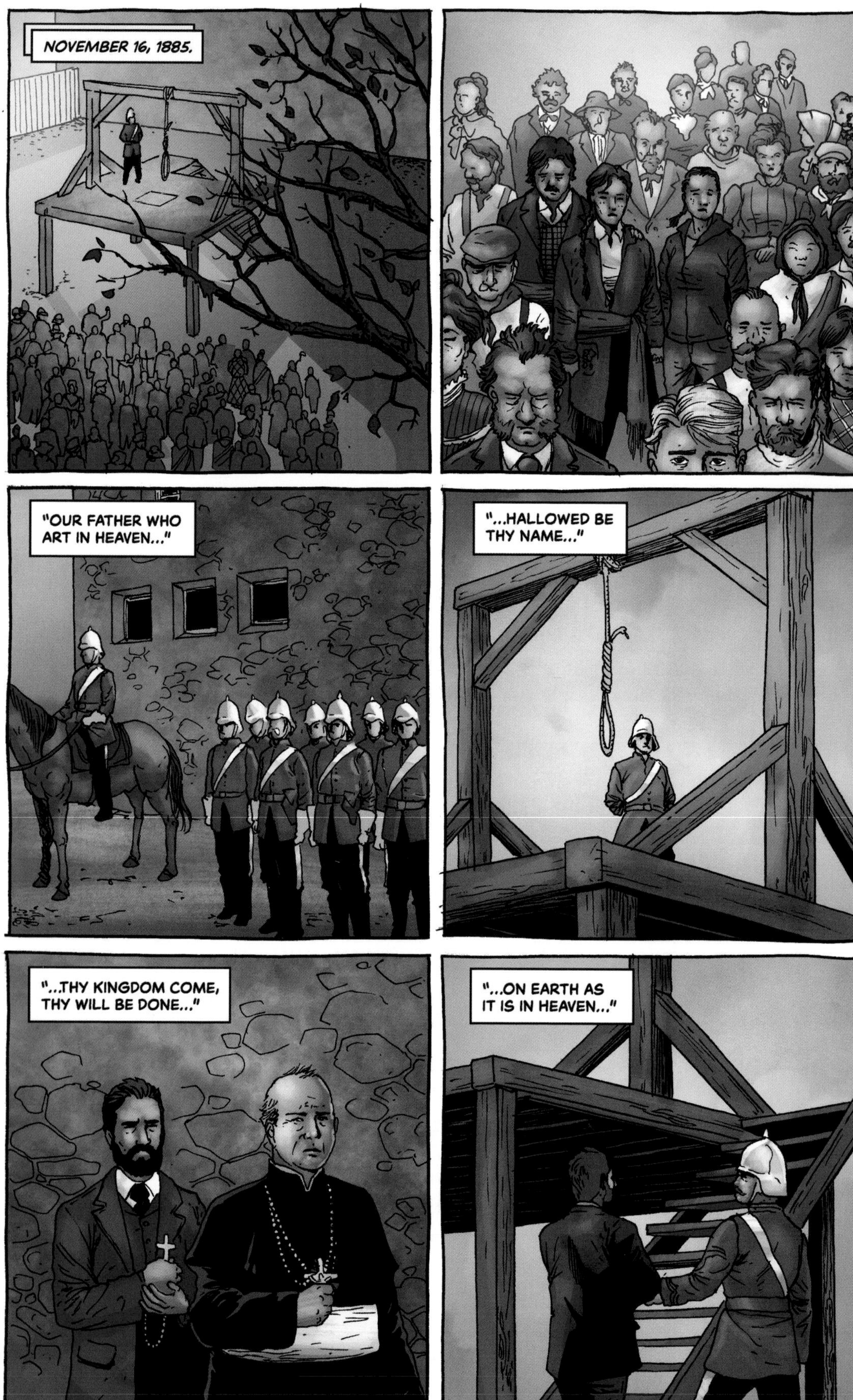
NOVEMBER 16, 1885.
"OUR FATHER WHO ART IN HEAVEN..."
"...HALLOWED BE THY NAME..."
"...THY KINGDOM COME, THY WILL BE DONE..."
"...ON EARTH AS IT IS IN HEAVEN..."

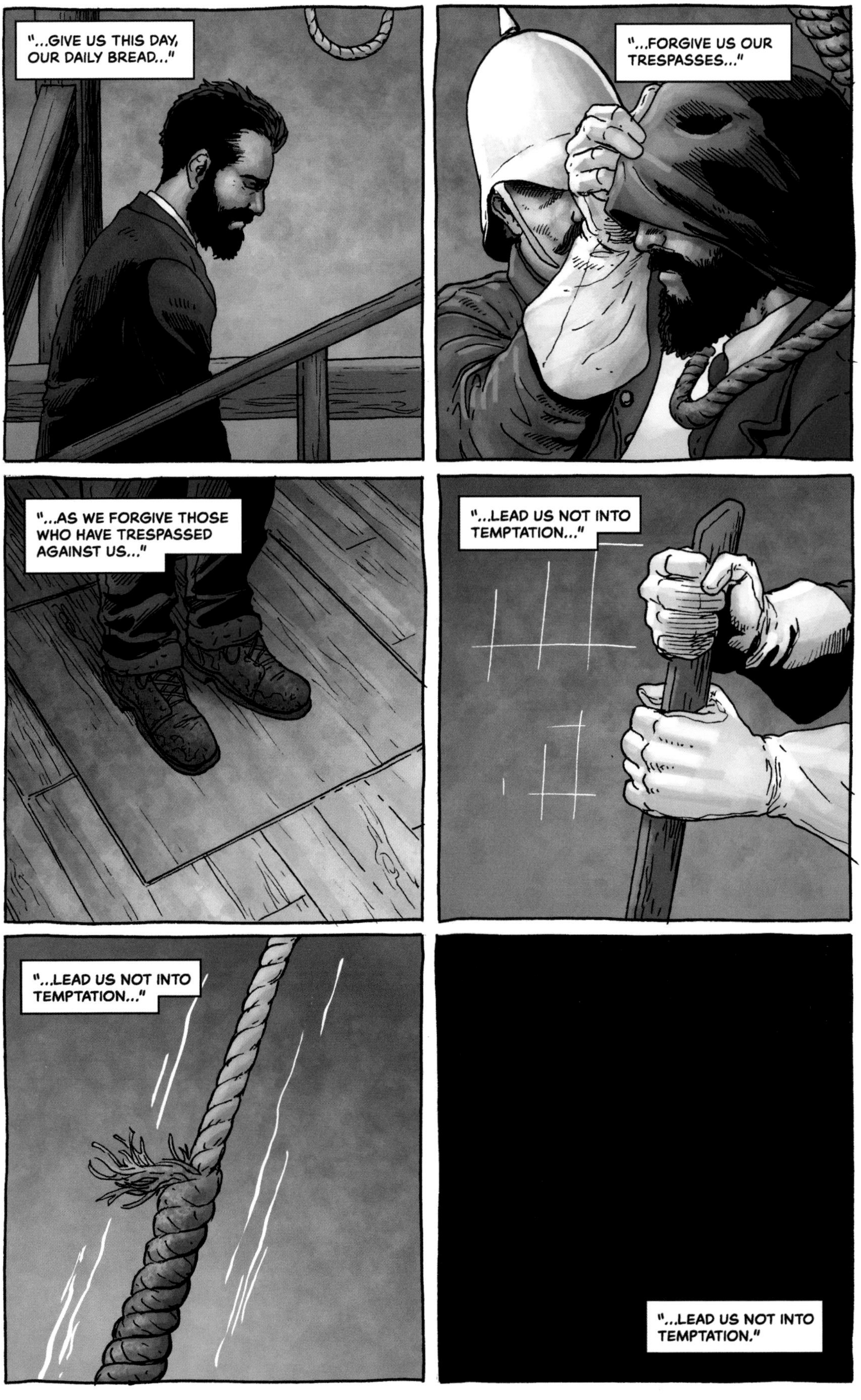
"...GIVE US THIS DAY, OUR DAILY BREAD..."
"...FORGIVE US OUR TRESPASSES..."
"...AS WE FORGIVE THOSE WHO HAVE TRESPASSED AGAINST US..."
"...LEAD US NOT INTO TEMPTATION..."
"...LEAD US NOT INTO TEMPTATION..."
"...LEAD US NOT INTO TEMPTATION."

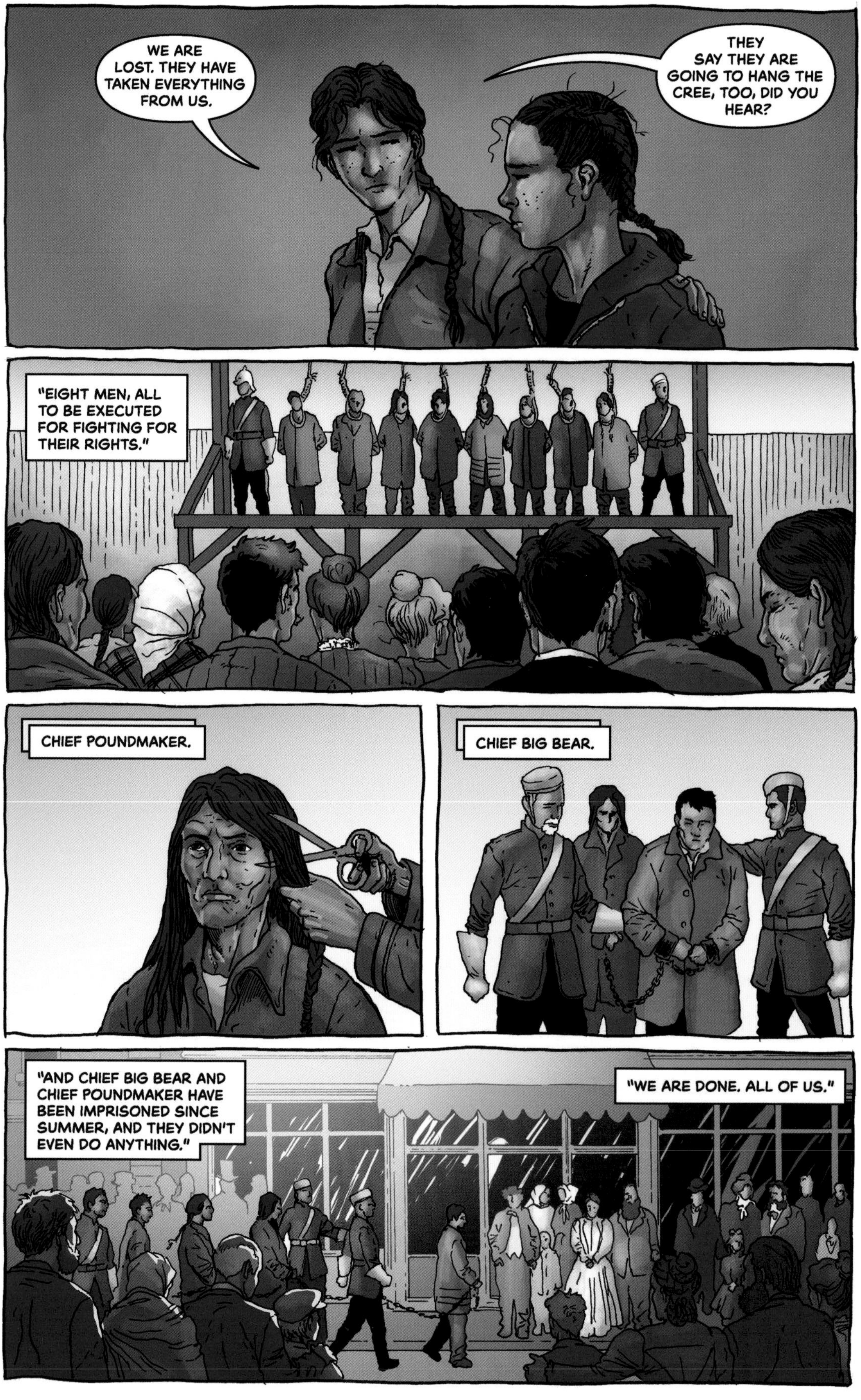
WE ARE LOST. THEY HAVE TAKEN EVERYTHING FROM US.
THEY SAY THEY ARE GOING TO HANG THE CREE, TOO, DID YOU HEAR?
"EIGHT MEN, ALL TO BE EXECUTED FOR FIGHTING FOR THEIR RIGHTS."
CHIEF POUNDMAKER.
CHIEF BIG BEAR.
"AND CHIEF BIG BEAR AND CHIEF POUNDMAKER HAVE BEEN IMPRISONED SINCE SUMMER, AND THEY DIDN'T EVEN DO ANYTHING."
"WE ARE DONE. ALL OF US."

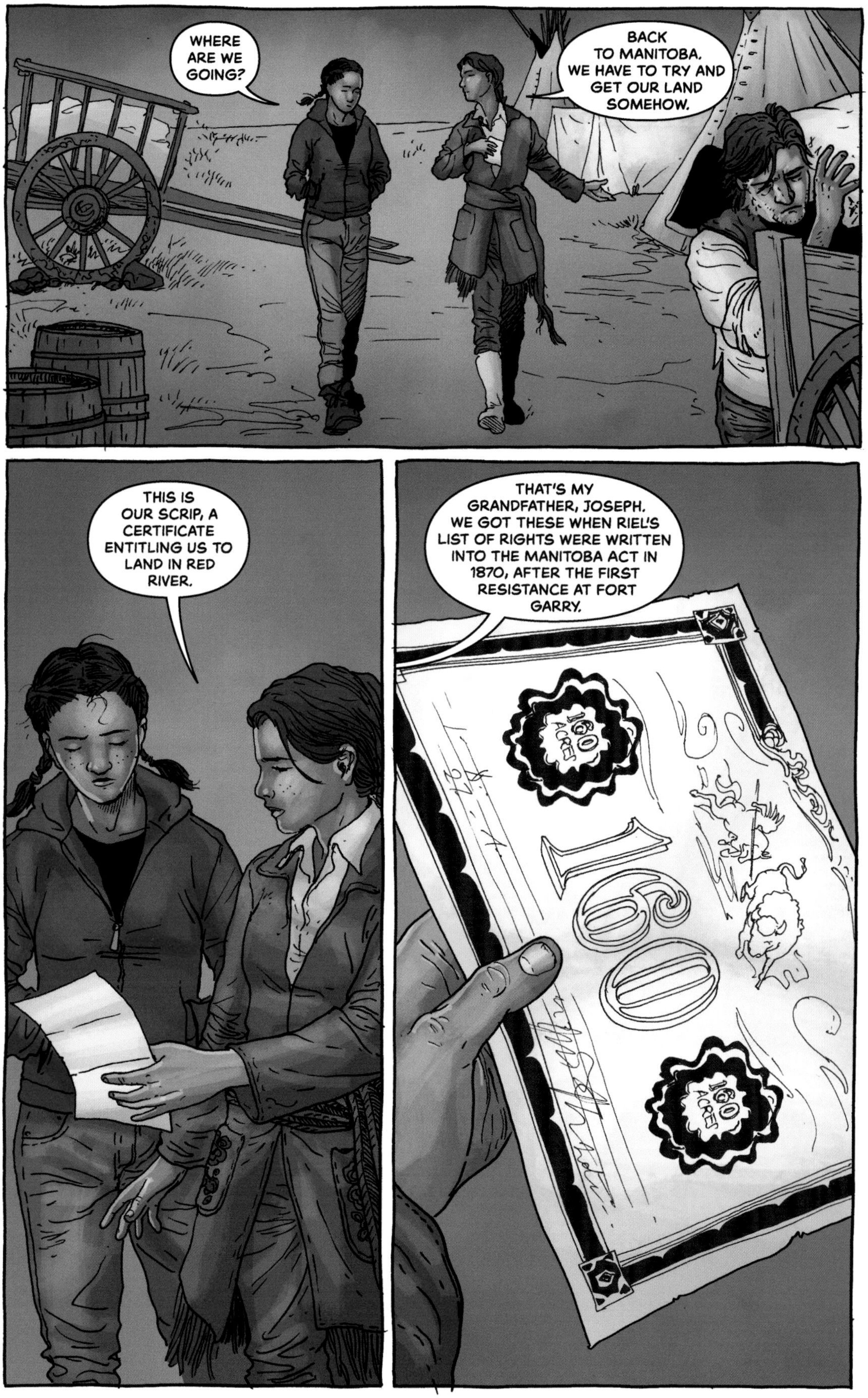
WHERE ARE WE GOING?
BACK TO MANITOBA. WE HAVE TO TRY AND GET OUR LAND SOMEHOW.
THIS IS OUR SCRIP, A CERTIFICATE ENTITLING US TO LAND IN RED RIVER.
THAT'S MY GRANDFATHER, JOSEPH. WE GOT THESE WHEN RIEL'S LIST OF RIGHTS WERE WRITTEN INTO THE MANITOBA ACT IN 1870, AFTER THE FIRST RESISTANCE AT FORT GARRY.

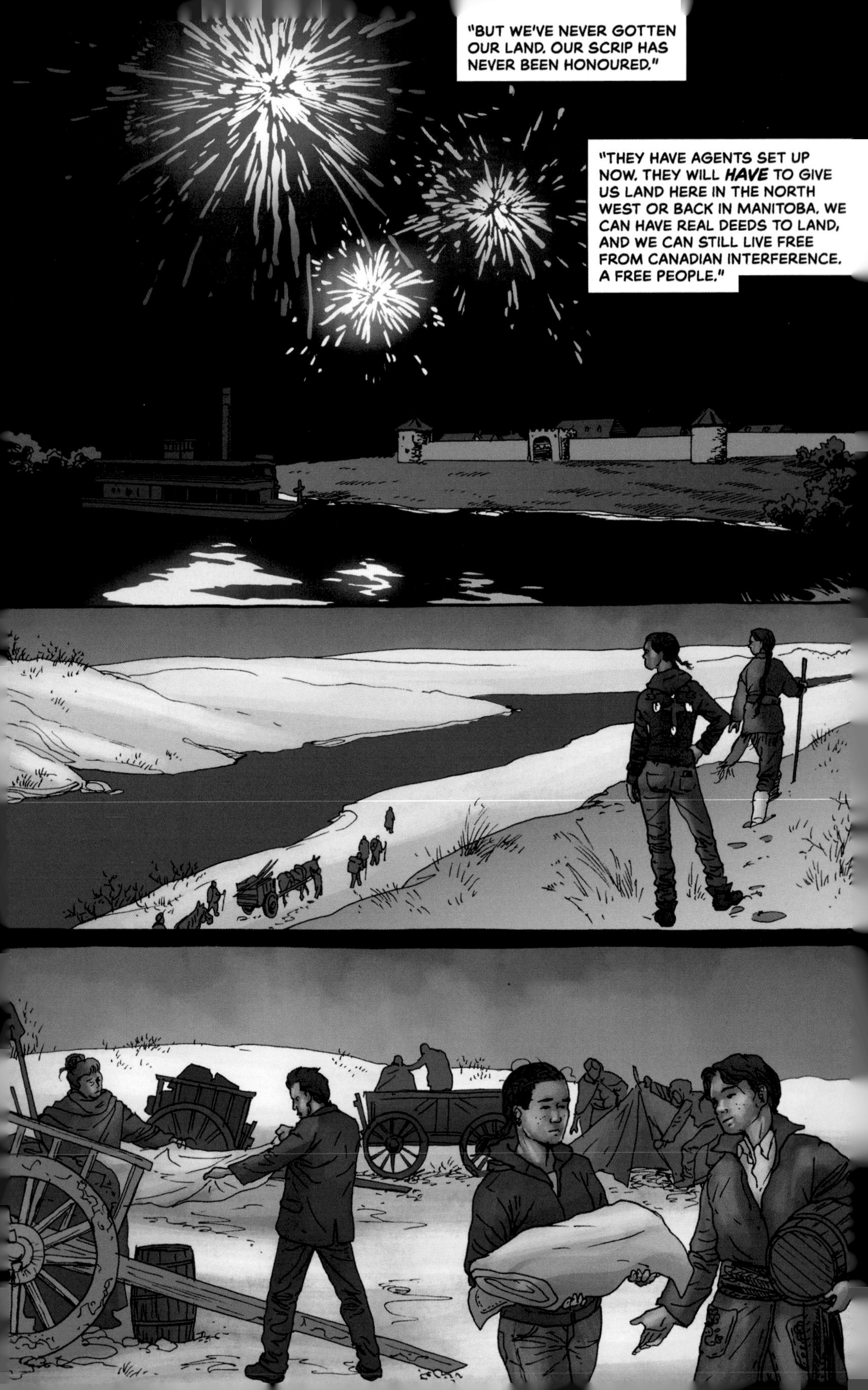
"BUT WE'VE NEVER GOTTEN OUR LAND. OUR SCRIP HAS NEVER BEEN HONOURED."
"THEY HAVE AGENTS SET UP NOW. THEY WILL HAVE TO GIVE US LAND HERE IN THE NORTH WEST OR BACK IN MANITOBA. WE CAN HAVE REAL DEEDS TO LAND, AND WE CAN STILL LIVE FREE FROM CANADIAN INTERFERENCE. A FREE PEOPLE."

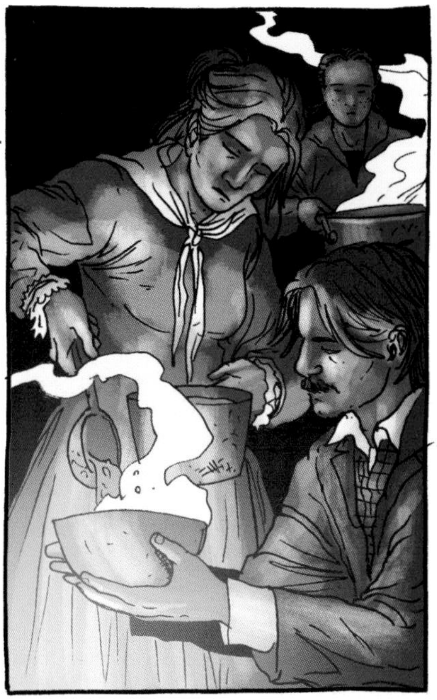
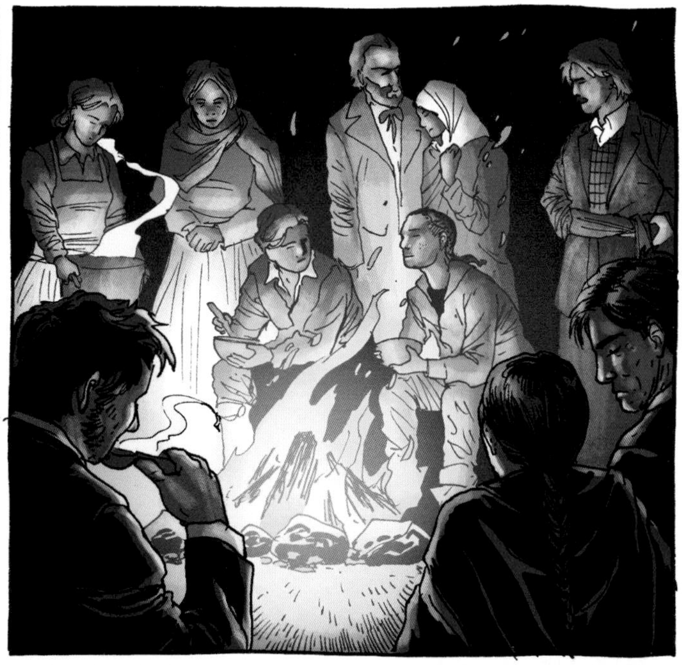
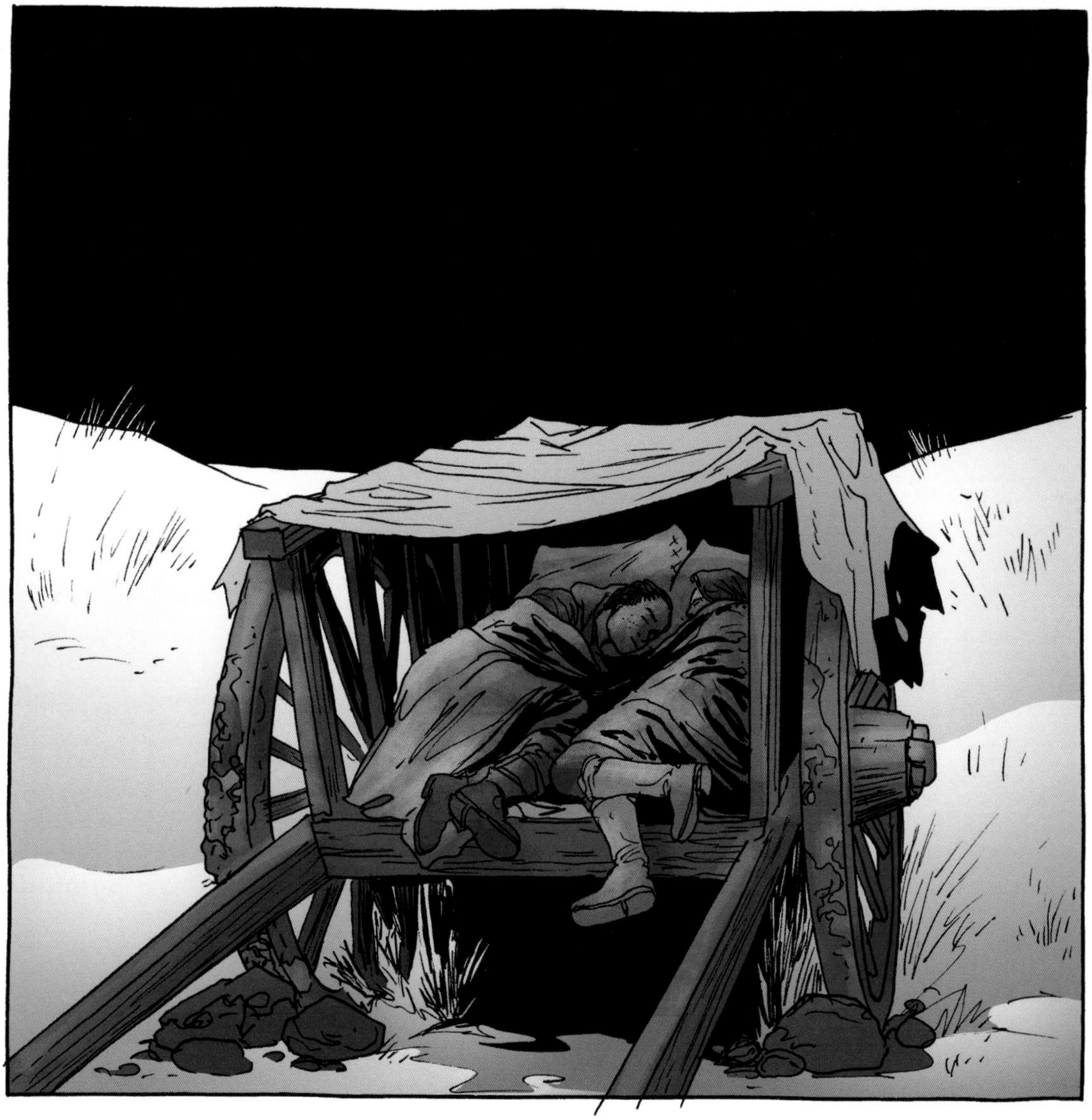

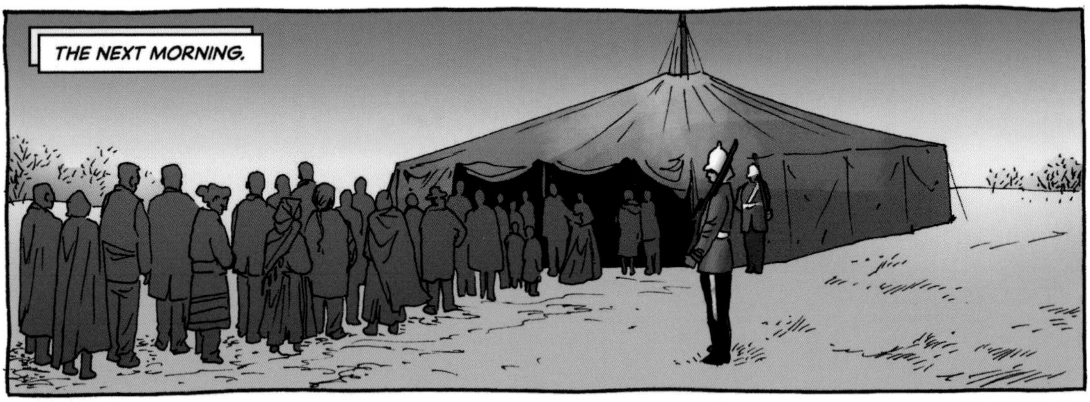
THE NEXT MORNING.

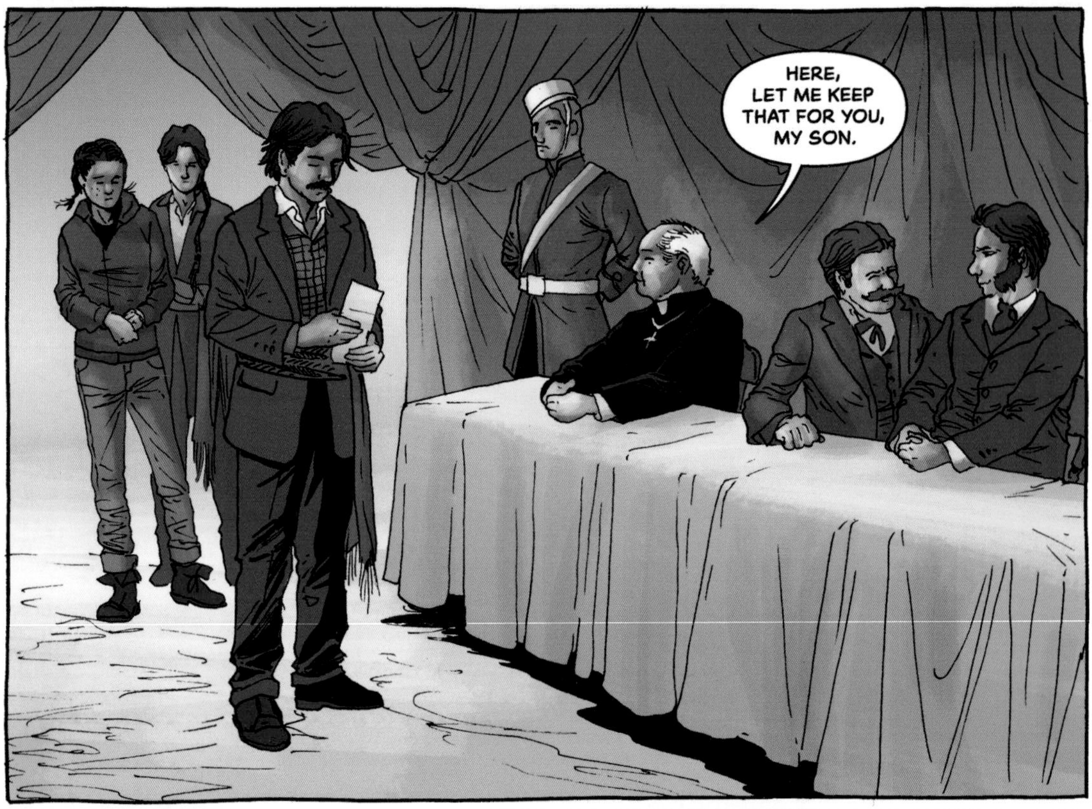
HERE, LET ME KEEP THAT FOR YOU, MY SON.

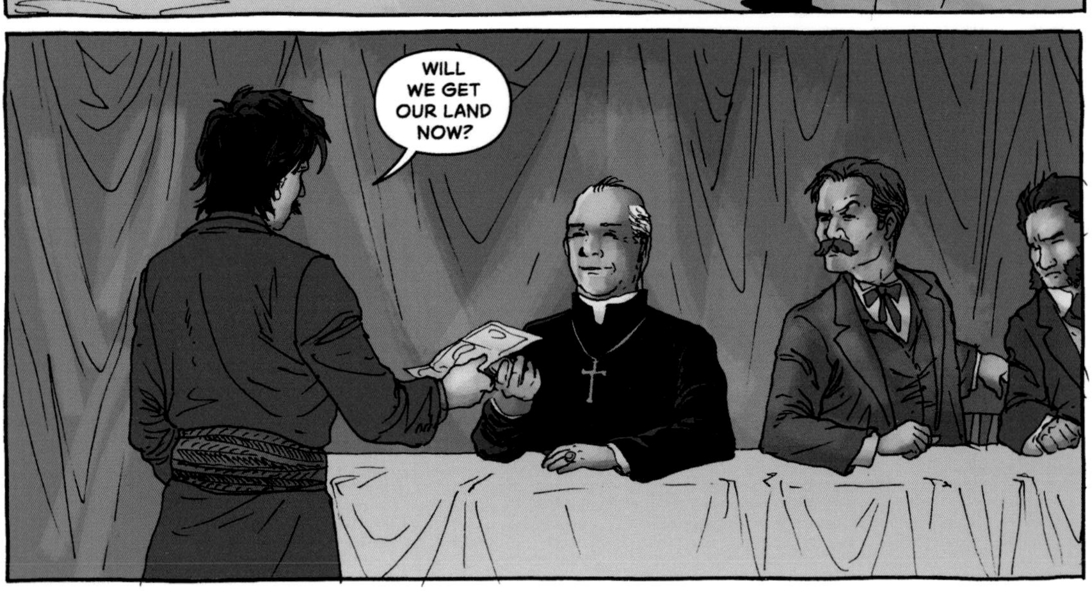
WILL WE GET OUR LAND NOW?

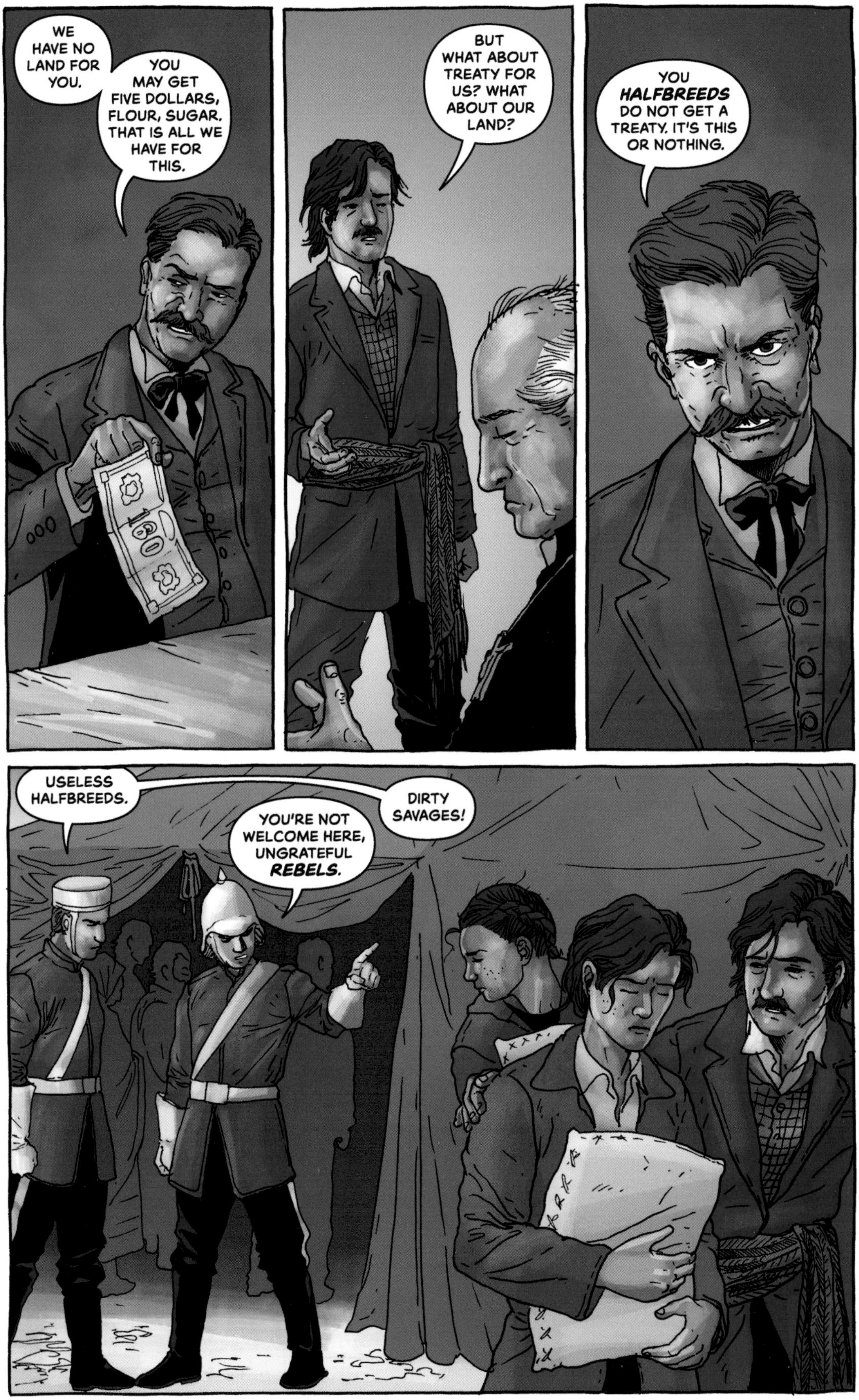
WE HAVE NO LAND FOR YOU.
YOU MAY GET FIVE DOLLARS, FLOUR, SUGAR. THAT IS ALL WE HAVE FOR THIS.
BUT WHAT ABOUT TREATY FOR US? WHAT ABOUT OUR LAND?
YOU *HALFBREEDS* DO NOT GET A TREATY. IT'S THIS OR NOTHING.
USELESS HALFBREEDS.
DIRTY SAVAGES!
YOU'RE NOT WELCOME HERE, UNGRATEFUL *REBELS.*

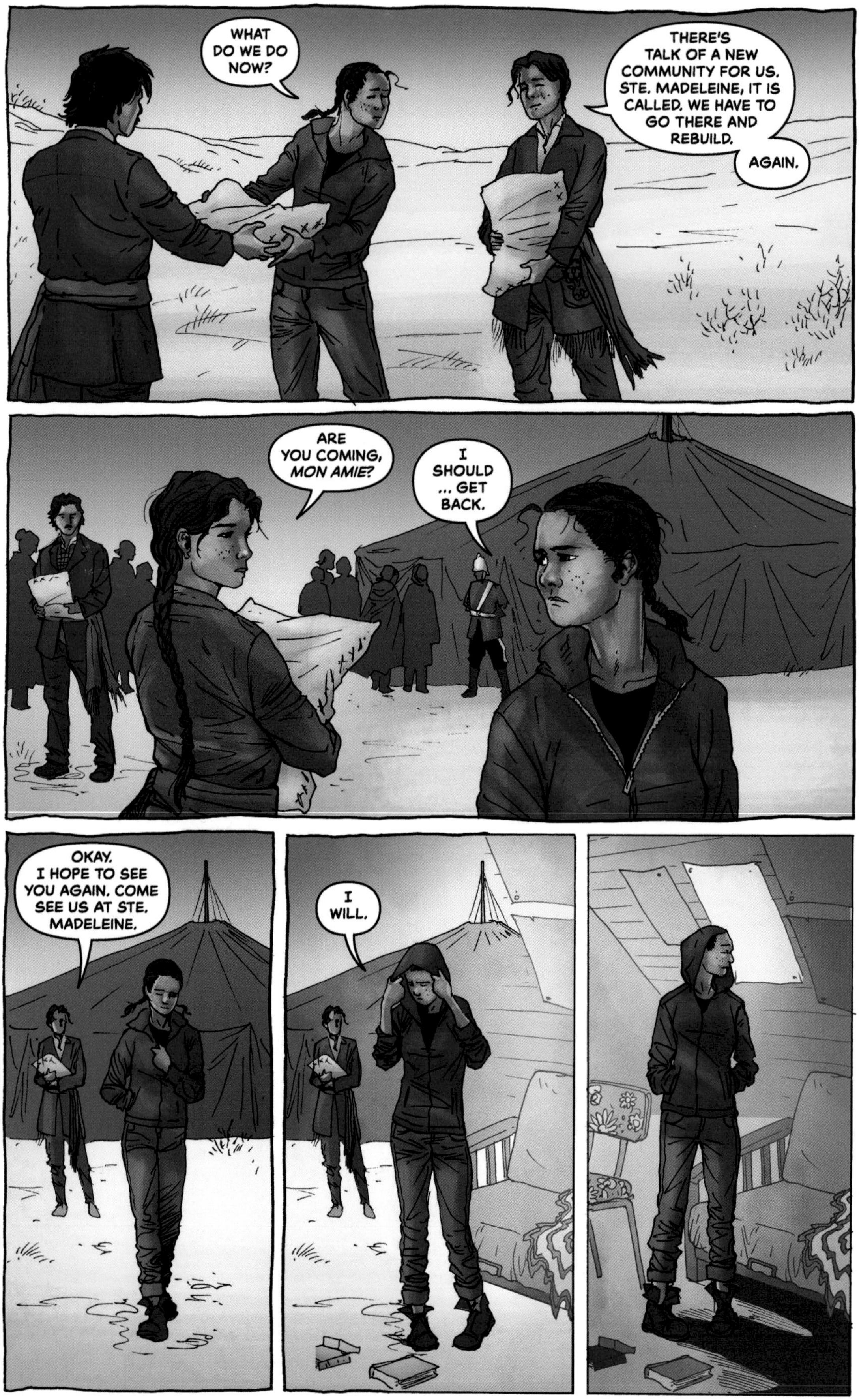
WHAT DO WE DO NOW?
THERE'S TALK OF A NEW COMMUNITY FOR US. STE. MADELEINE, IT IS CALLED. WE HAVE TO GO THERE AND REBUILD.
AGAIN.
ARE YOU COMING, *MON AMIE?*
I SHOULD ... GET BACK.
OKAY. I HOPE TO SEE YOU AGAIN. COME SEE US AT STE. MADELEINE.
I WILL.

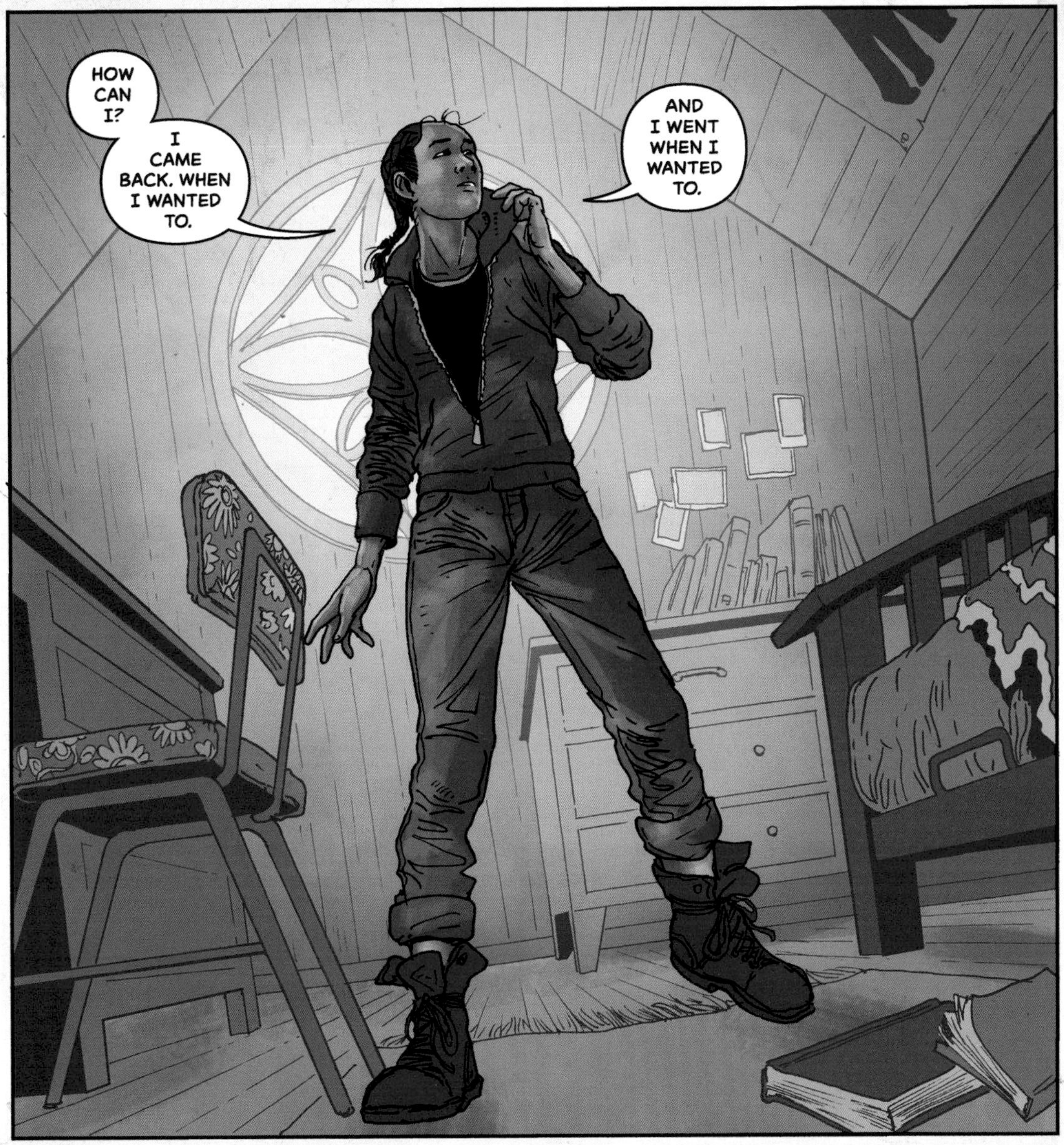
HOW CAN I?
I CAME BACK. WHEN I WANTED TO.
AND I WENT WHEN I WANTED TO.

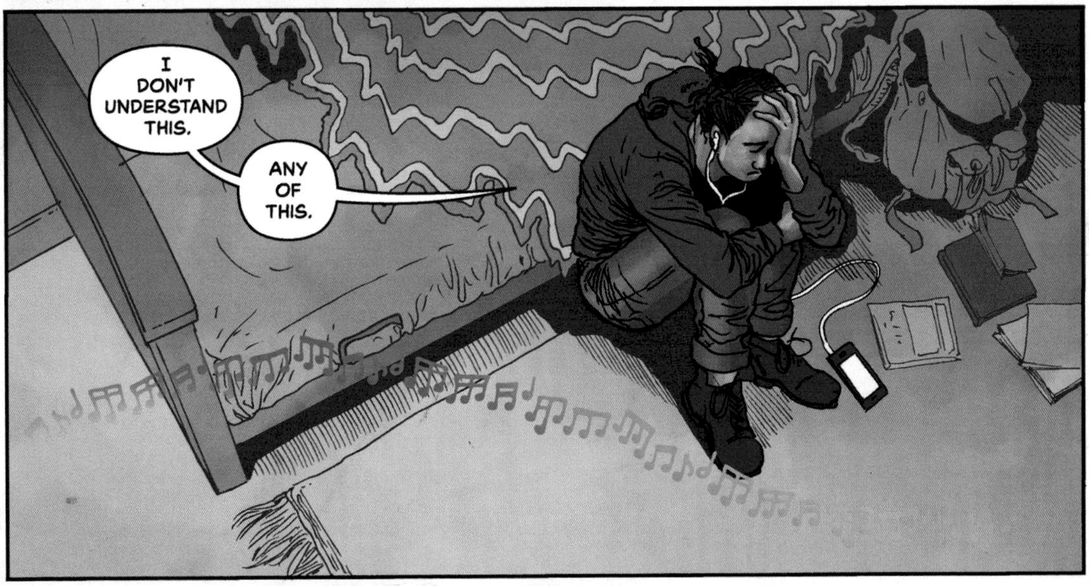
I DON'T UNDERSTAND THIS.
ANY OF THIS.

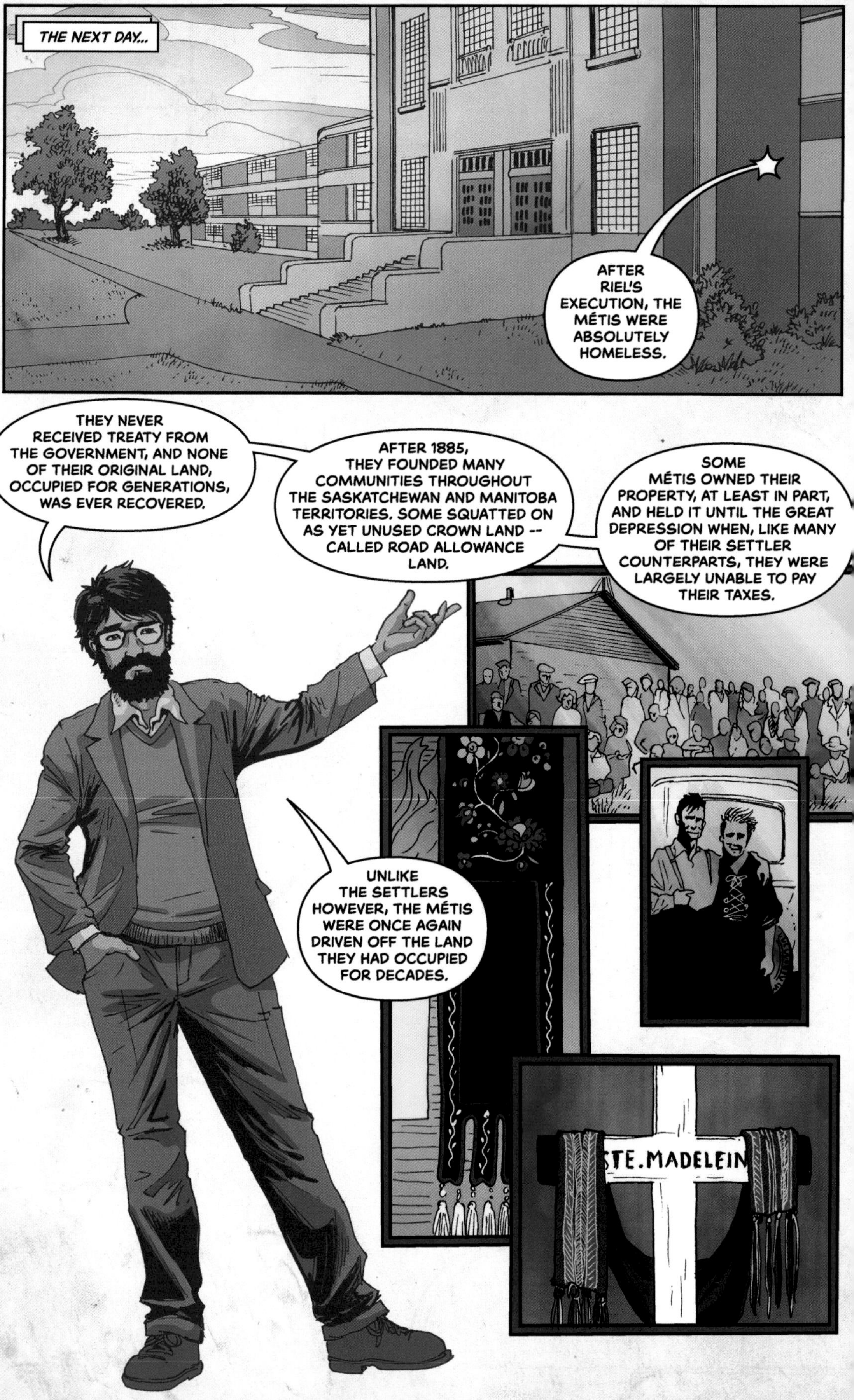
THE NEXT DAY...
AFTER RIEL'S EXECUTION, THE MÉTIS WERE ABSOLUTELY HOMELESS.
THEY NEVER RECEIVED TREATY FROM THE GOVERNMENT, AND NONE OF THEIR ORIGINAL LAND, OCCUPIED FOR GENERATIONS, WAS EVER RECOVERED.
AFTER 1885, THEY FOUNDED MANY COMMUNITIES THROUGHOUT THE SASKATCHEWAN AND MANITOBA TERRITORIES. SOME SQUATTED ON AS YET UNUSED CROWN LAND -- CALLED ROAD ALLOWANCE LAND.
SOME MÉTIS OWNED THEIR PROPERTY, AT LEAST IN PART, AND HELD IT UNTIL THE GREAT DEPRESSION WHEN, LIKE MANY OF THEIR SETTLER COUNTERPARTS, THEY WERE LARGELY UNABLE TO PAY THEIR TAXES.
UNLIKE THE SETTLERS HOWEVER, THE MÉTIS WERE ONCE AGAIN DRIVEN OFF THE LAND THEY HAD OCCUPIED FOR DECADES.
STE. MADELEIN

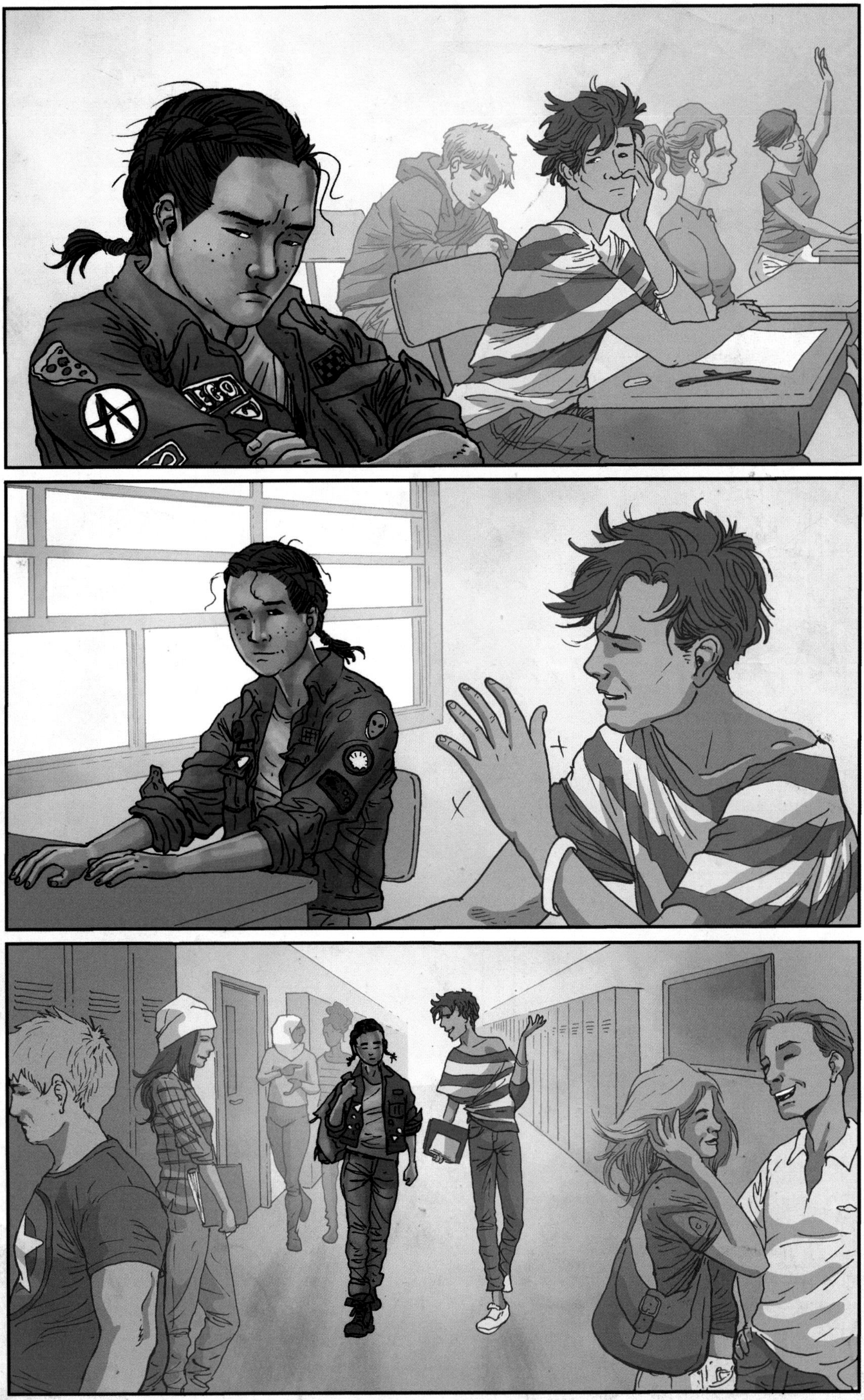

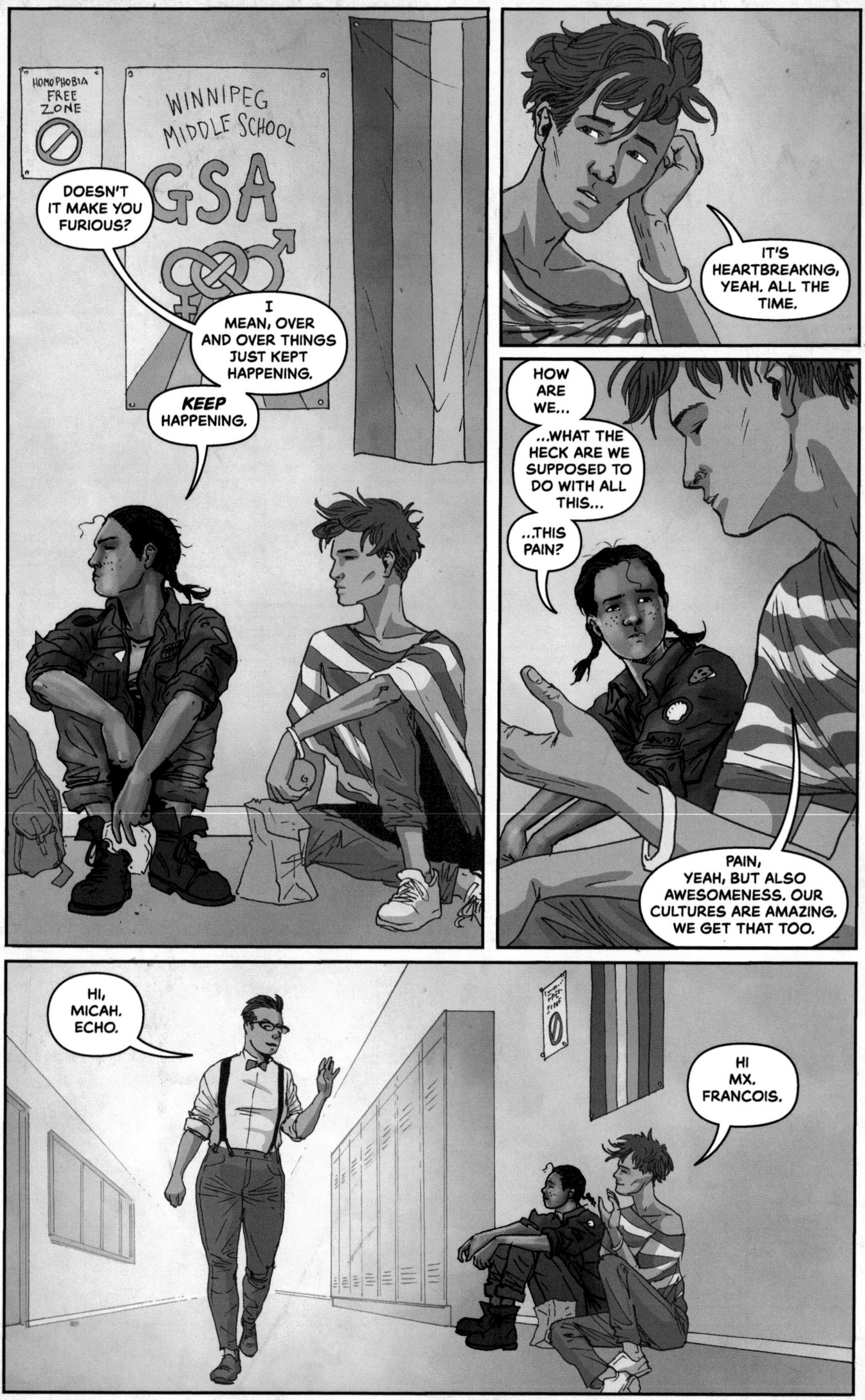
HOMOPHOBIA FREE ZONE
WINNIPEG MIDDLE SCHOOL GSA
DOESN'T IT MAKE YOU FURIOUS?
I MEAN, OVER AND OVER THINGS JUST KEPT HAPPENING.
KEEP HAPPENING.
IT'S HEARTBREAKING, YEAH. ALL THE TIME.
HOW ARE WE...
...WHAT THE HECK ARE WE SUPPOSED TO DO WITH ALL THIS...
...THIS PAIN?
PAIN, YEAH, BUT ALSO AWESOMENESS. OUR CULTURES ARE AMAZING. WE GET THAT TOO.
HI, MICAH. ECHO.
HI MX. FRANCOIS.

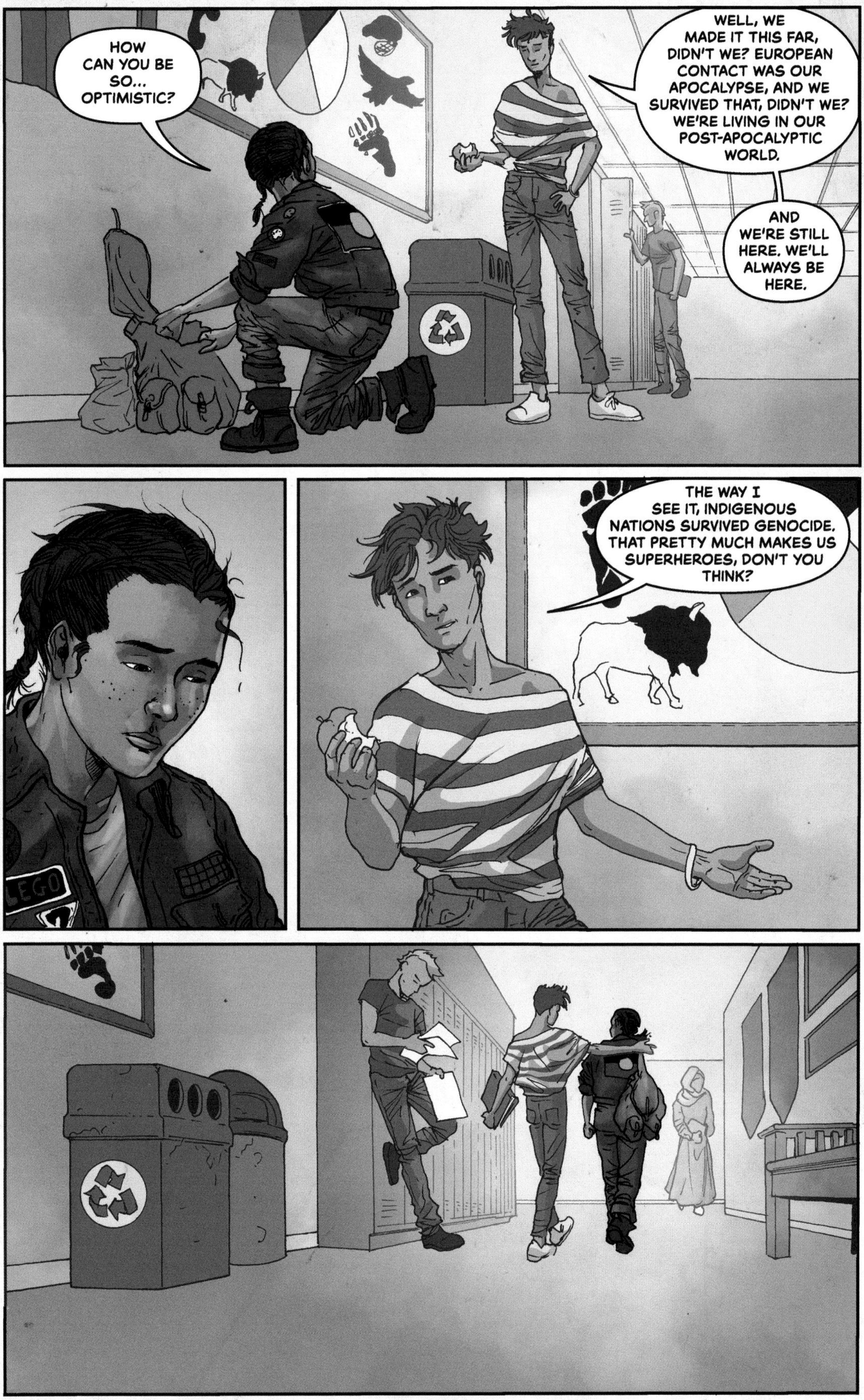
HOW CAN YOU BE SO... OPTIMISTIC?
WELL, WE MADE IT THIS FAR, DIDN'T WE? EUROPEAN CONTACT WAS OUR APOCALYPSE, AND WE SURVIVED THAT, DIDN'T WE? WE'RE LIVING IN OUR POST-APOCALYPTIC WORLD.
AND WE'RE STILL HERE. WE'LL ALWAYS BE HERE.
THE WAY I SEE IT, INDIGENOUS NATIONS SURVIVED GENOCIDE. THAT PRETTY MUCH MAKES US SUPERHEROES, DON'T YOU THINK?

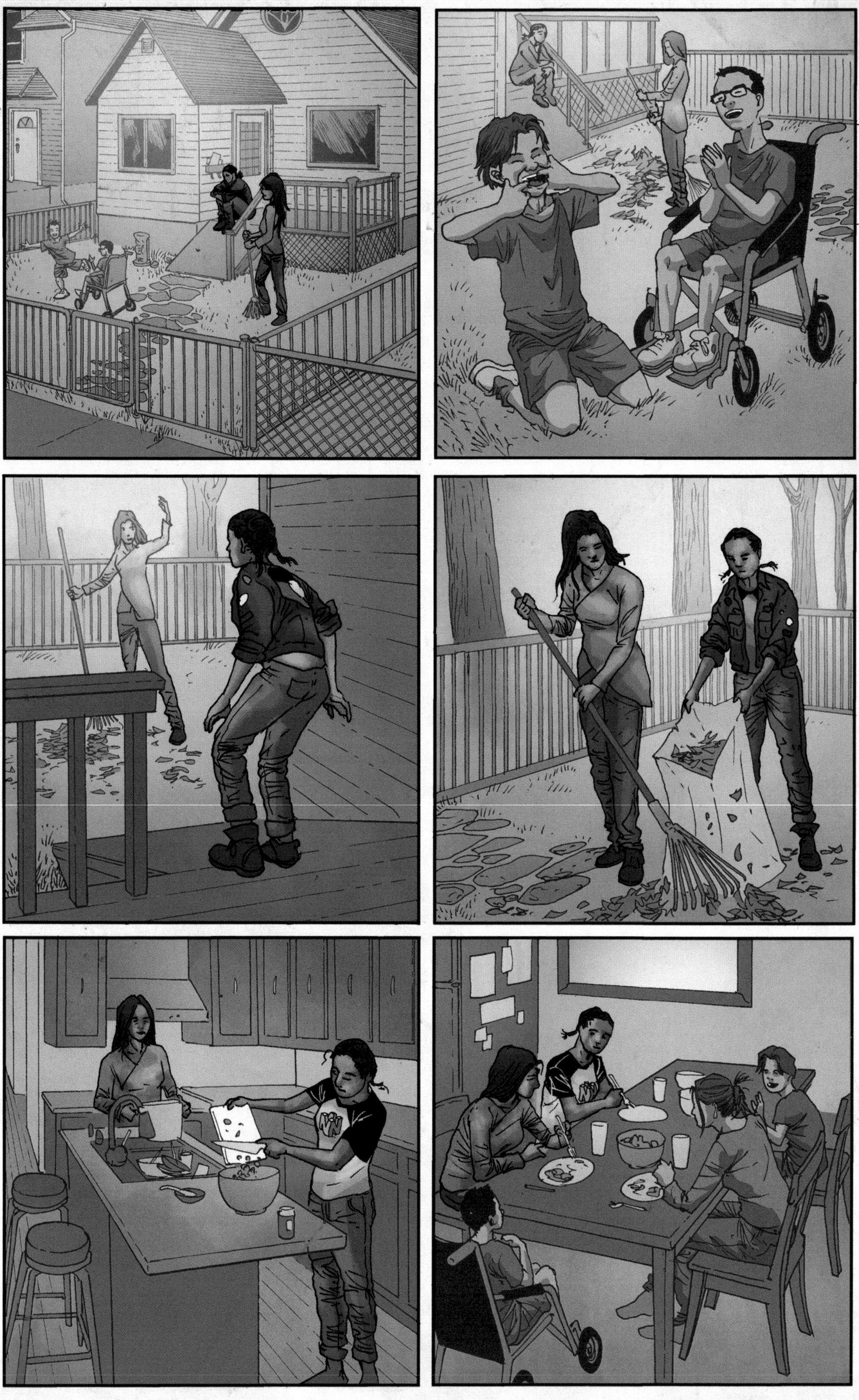

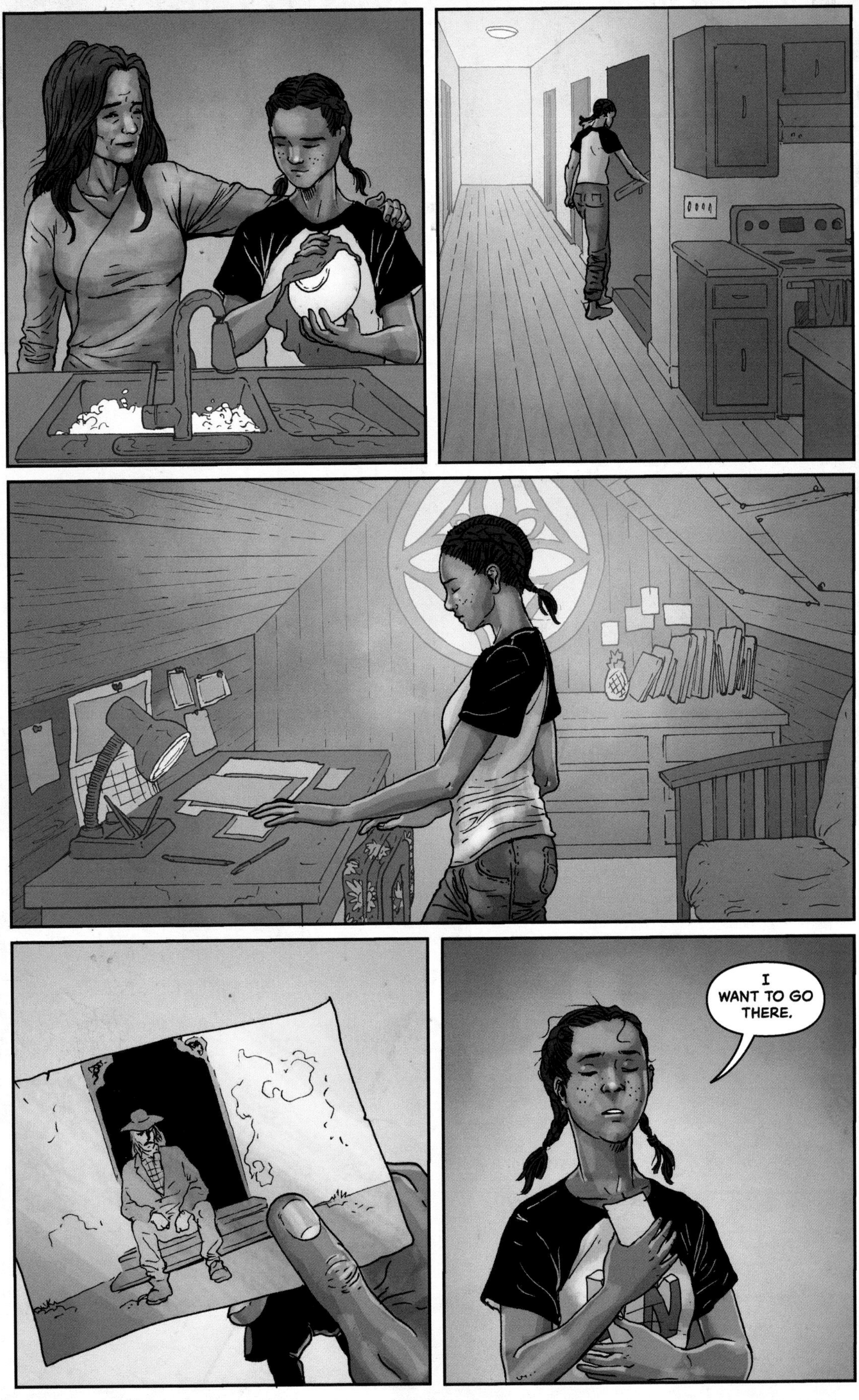
I WANT TO GO THERE.

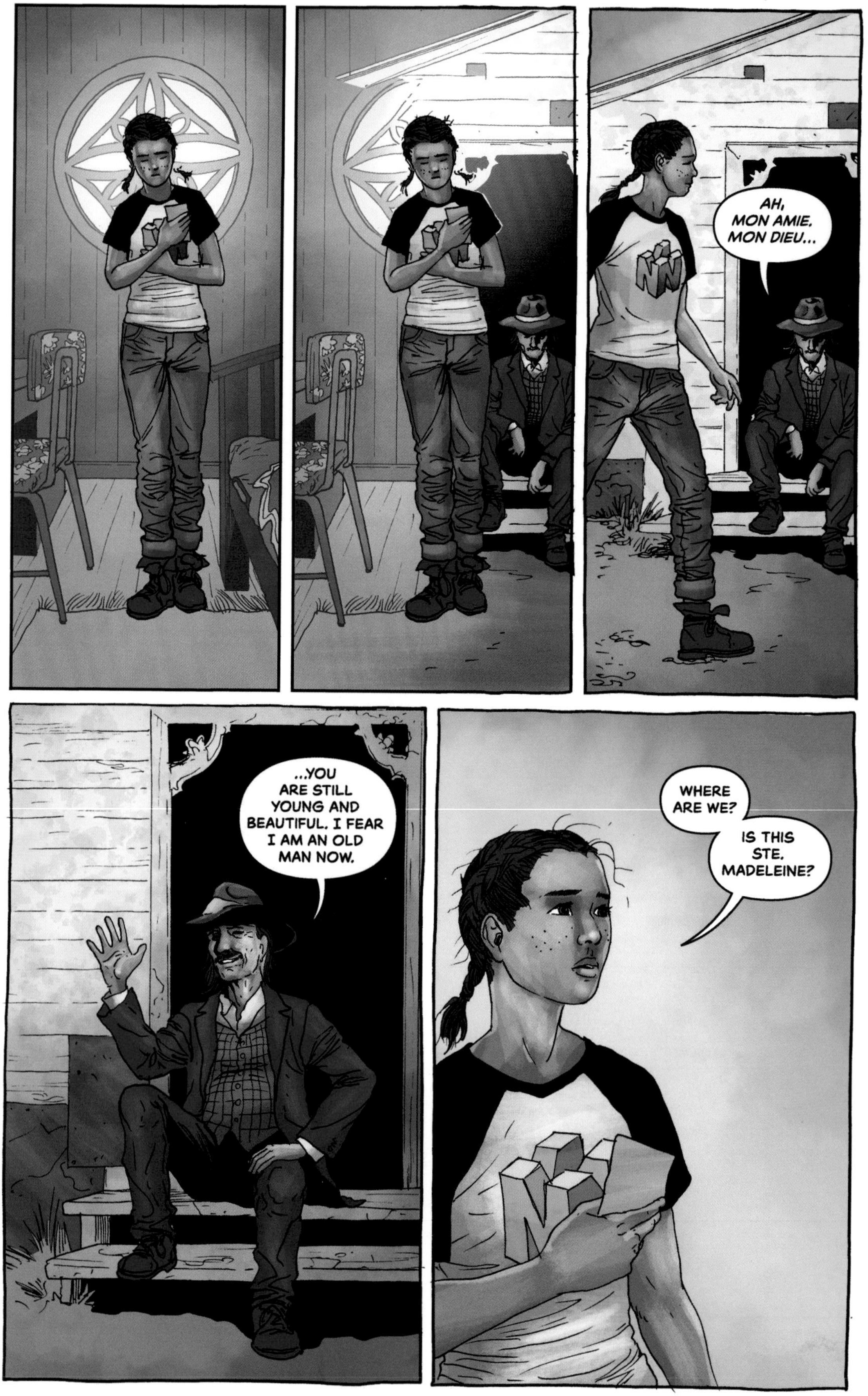
AH,
MON AMIE.
MON DIEU...
...YOU
ARE STILL
YOUNG AND
BEAUTIFUL. I FEAR
I AM AN OLD
MAN NOW.
WHERE
ARE WE?
IS THIS
STE.
MADELEINE?

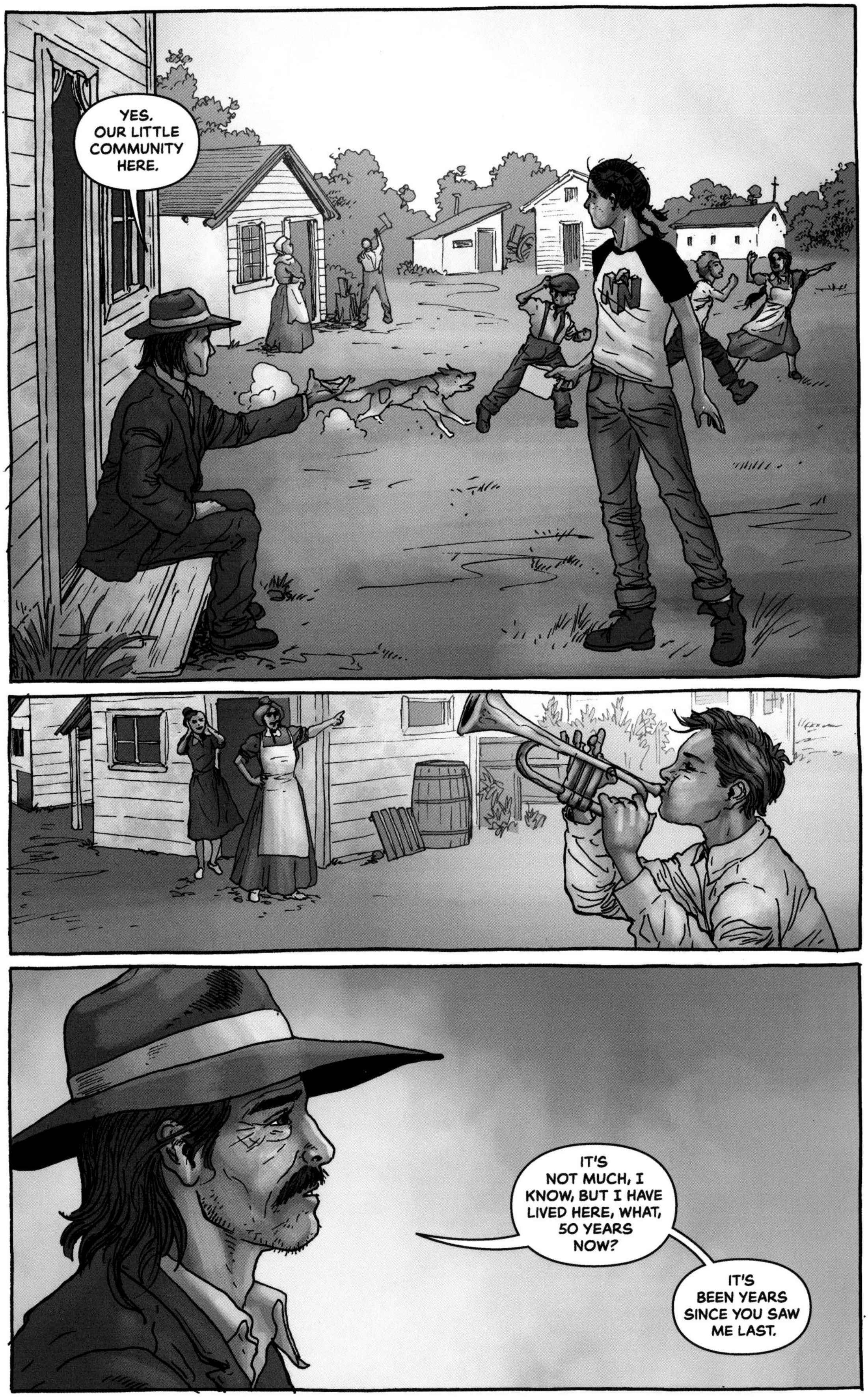
YES. OUR LITTLE COMMUNITY HERE.
IT'S NOT MUCH, I KNOW, BUT I HAVE LIVED HERE, WHAT, 50 YEARS NOW?
IT'S BEEN YEARS SINCE YOU SAW ME LAST.

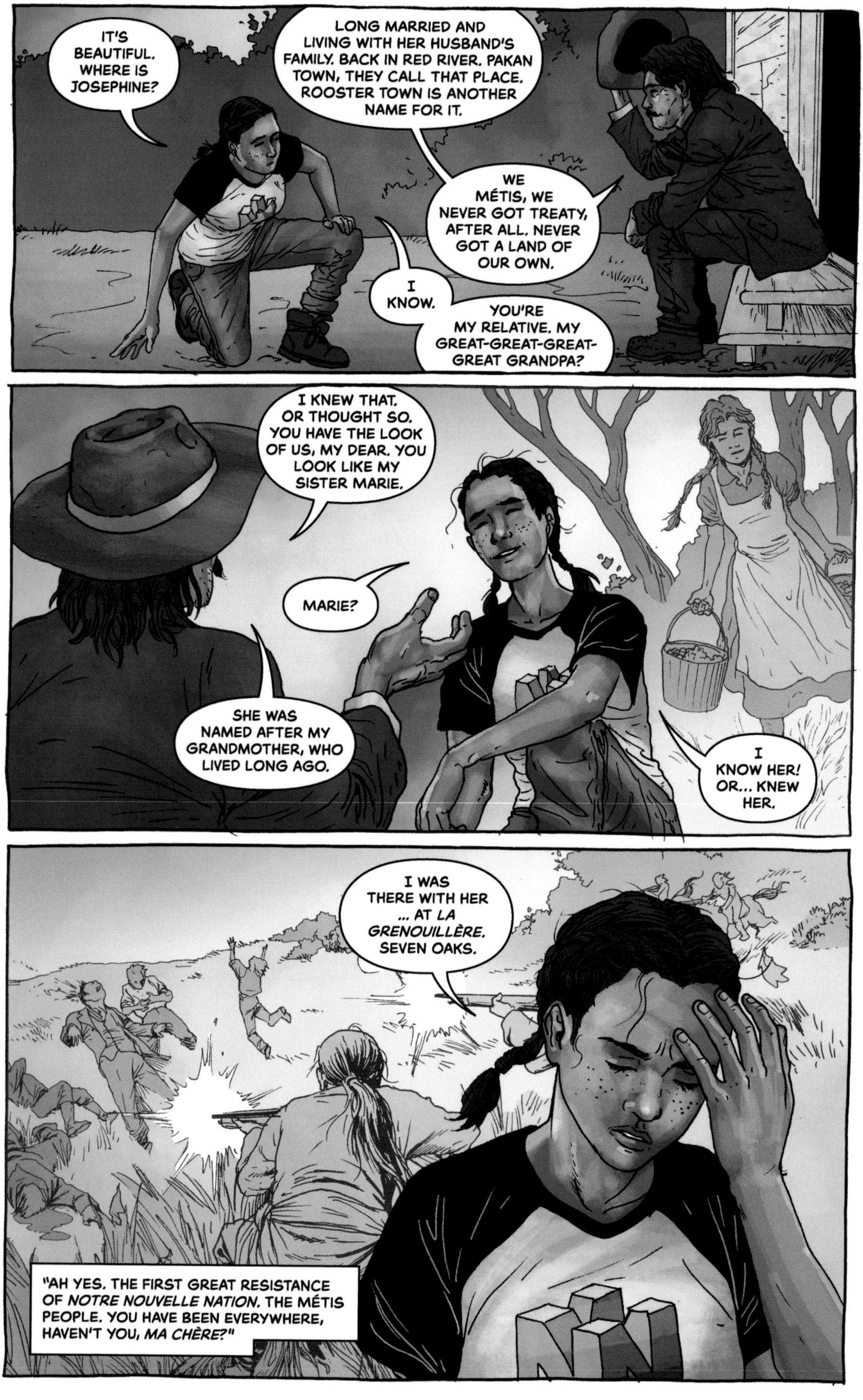
IT'S BEAUTIFUL. WHERE IS JOSEPHINE?
LONG MARRIED AND LIVING WITH HER HUSBAND'S FAMILY. BACK IN RED RIVER. PAKAN TOWN, THEY CALL THAT PLACE. ROOSTER TOWN IS ANOTHER NAME FOR IT.
WE MÉTIS, WE NEVER GOT TREATY, AFTER ALL. NEVER GOT A LAND OF OUR OWN.
I KNOW.
YOU'RE MY RELATIVE. MY GREAT-GREAT-GREAT-GREAT GRANDPA?
I KNEW THAT. OR THOUGHT SO. YOU HAVE THE LOOK OF US, MY DEAR. YOU LOOK LIKE MY SISTER MARIE.
MARIE?
SHE WAS NAMED AFTER MY GRANDMOTHER, WHO LIVED LONG AGO.
I KNOW HER! OR... KNEW HER.
I WAS THERE WITH HER ... AT *LA GRENOUILLÈRE*. SEVEN OAKS.
"AH YES. THE FIRST GREAT RESISTANCE OF *NOTRE NOUVELLE NATION*. THE MÉTIS PEOPLE. YOU HAVE BEEN EVERYWHERE, HAVEN'T YOU, *MA CHÈRE?*"

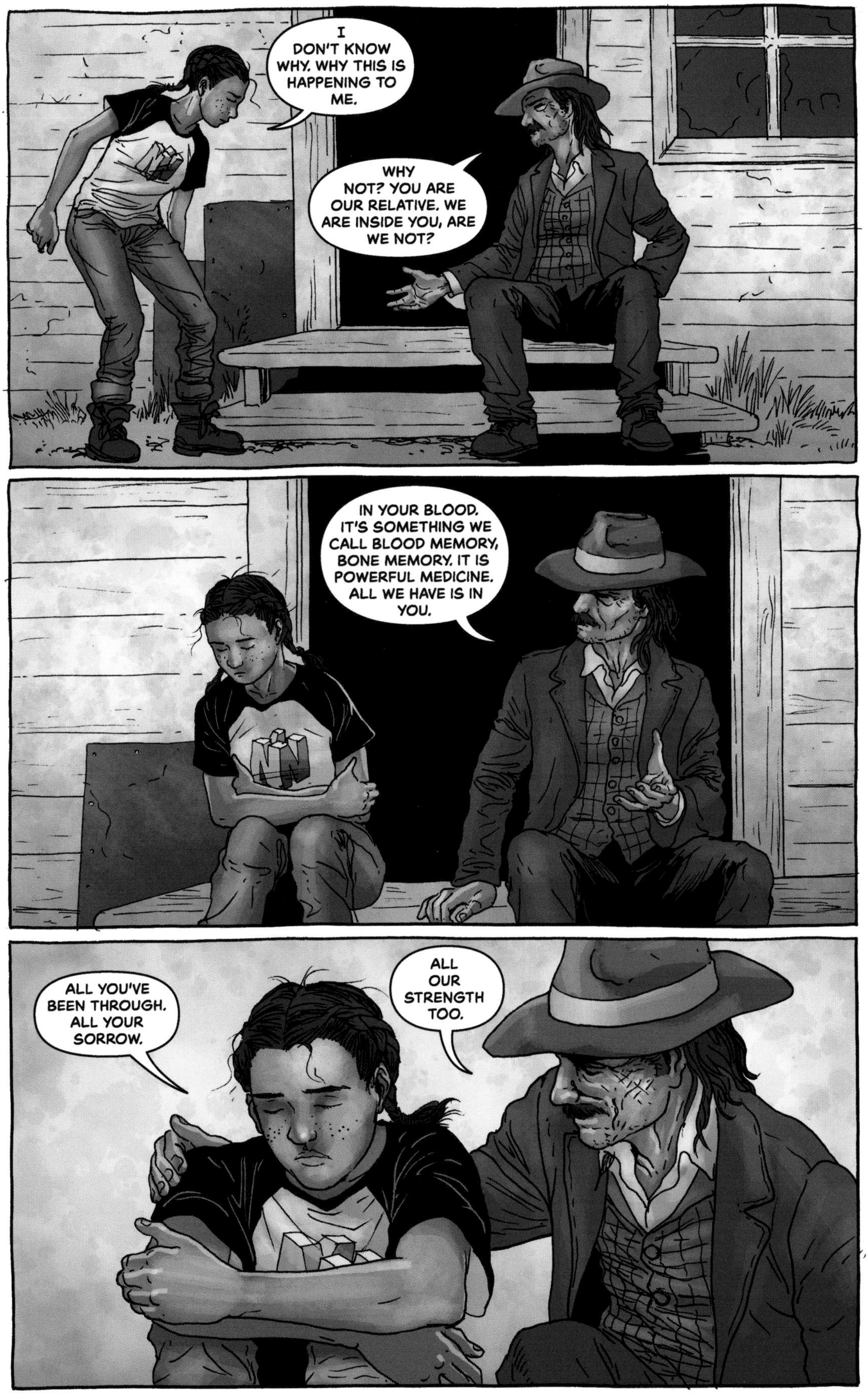
I DON'T KNOW WHY. WHY THIS IS HAPPENING TO ME.
WHY NOT? YOU ARE OUR RELATIVE. WE ARE INSIDE YOU, ARE WE NOT?
IN YOUR BLOOD. IT'S SOMETHING WE CALL BLOOD MEMORY, BONE MEMORY. IT IS POWERFUL MEDICINE. ALL WE HAVE IS IN YOU.
ALL YOU'VE BEEN THROUGH. ALL YOUR SORROW.
ALL OUR STRENGTH TOO.

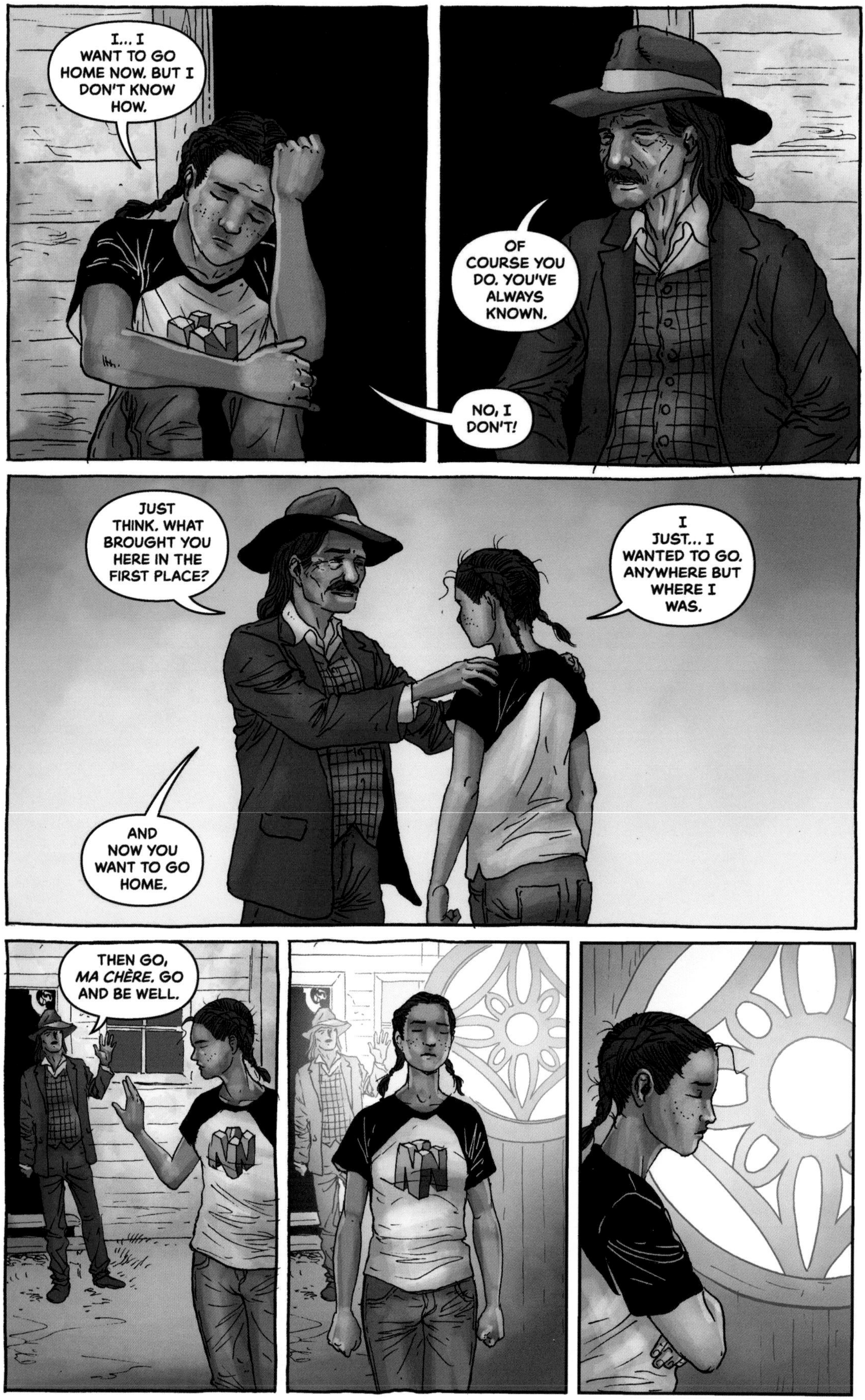

I... I WANT TO GO HOME NOW. BUT I DON'T KNOW HOW.
OF COURSE YOU DO. YOU'VE ALWAYS KNOWN.
NO, I DON'T!
JUST THINK. WHAT BROUGHT YOU HERE IN THE FIRST PLACE?
I JUST... I WANTED TO GO. ANYWHERE BUT WHERE I WAS.
AND NOW YOU WANT TO GO HOME.
THEN GO, *MA CHÈRE*. GO AND BE WELL.

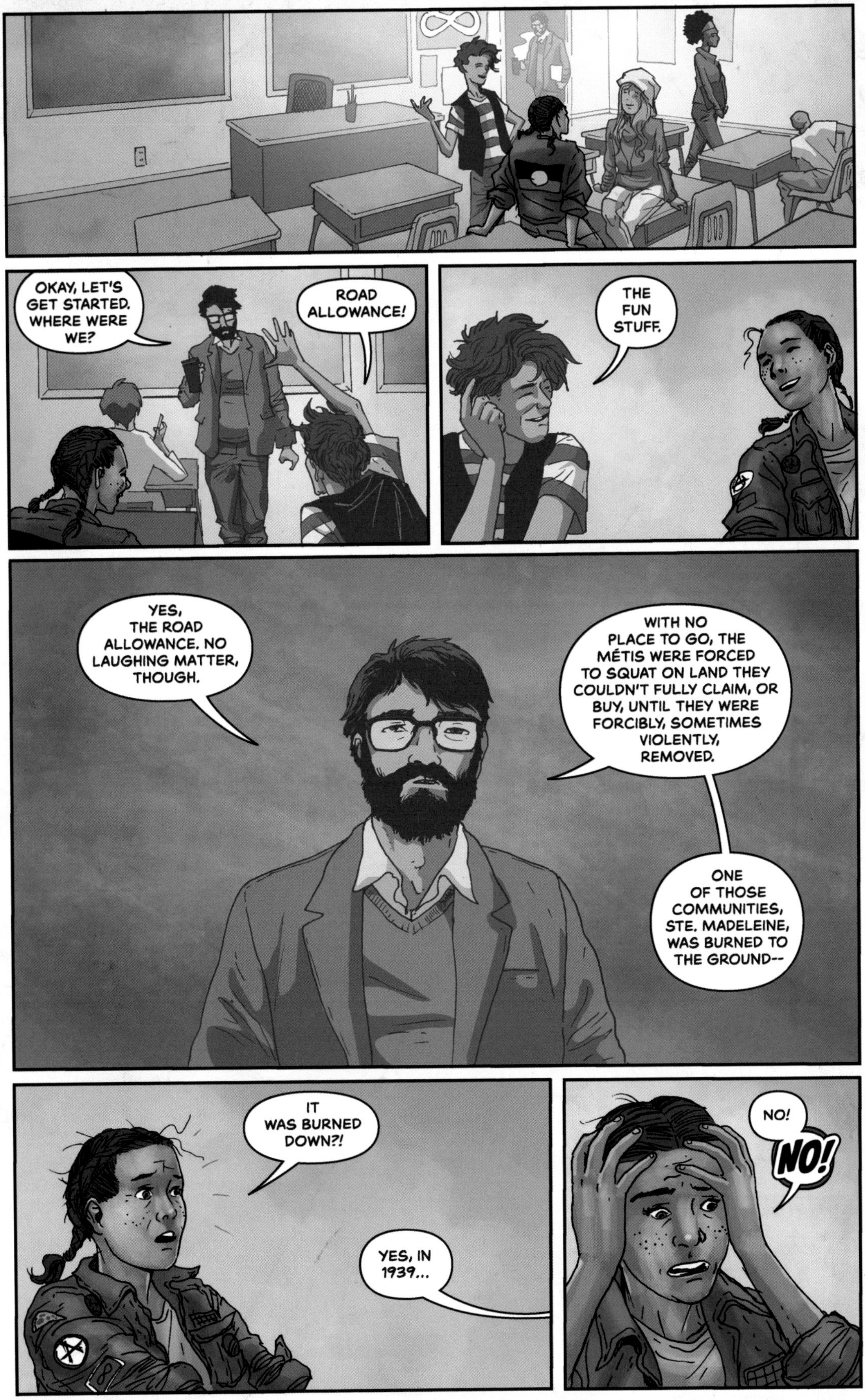
OKAY, LET'S GET STARTED. WHERE WERE WE?
ROAD ALLOWANCE!
THE FUN STUFF.
YES, THE ROAD ALLOWANCE. NO LAUGHING MATTER, THOUGH.
WITH NO PLACE TO GO, THE MÉTIS WERE FORCED TO SQUAT ON LAND THEY COULDN'T FULLY CLAIM, OR BUY, UNTIL THEY WERE FORCIBLY, SOMETIMES VIOLENTLY, REMOVED.
ONE OF THOSE COMMUNITIES, STE. MADELEINE, WAS BURNED TO THE GROUND--
IT WAS BURNED DOWN?!
YES, IN 1939...
NO!
NO!

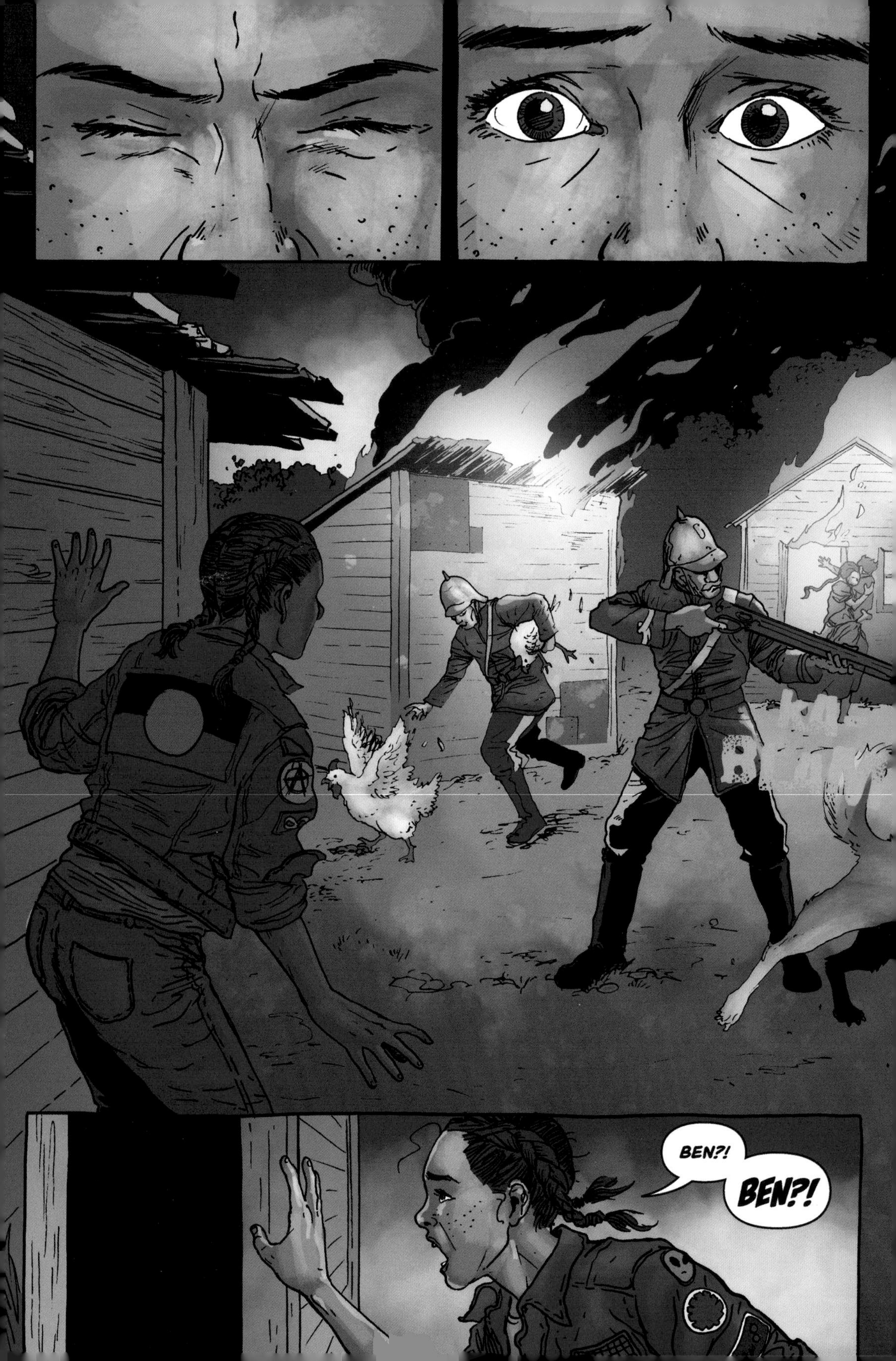
BEN?!
BEN?!

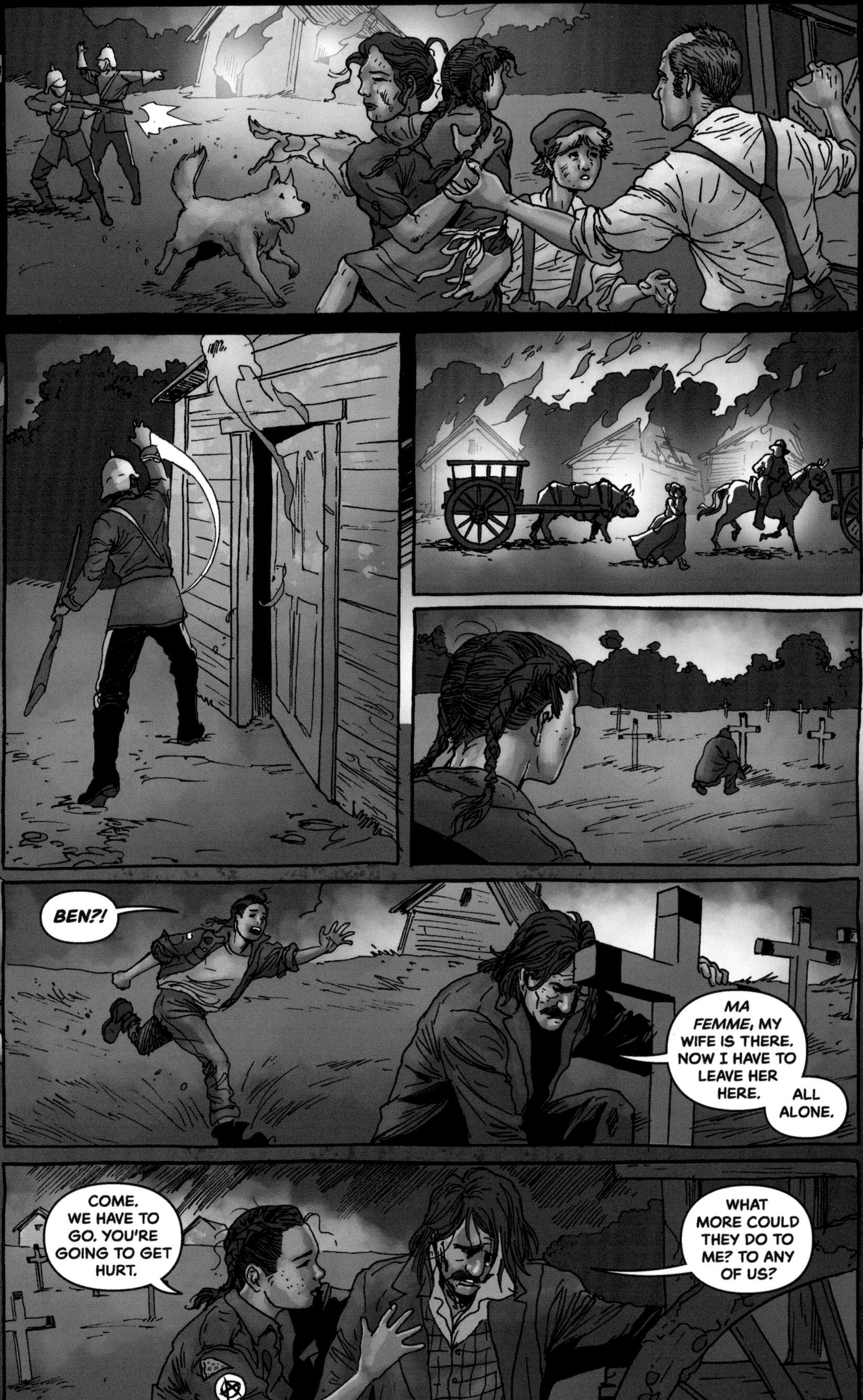
BEN?!
MA FEMME, MY WIFE IS THERE. NOW I HAVE TO LEAVE HER HERE.
ALL ALONE.
COME. WE HAVE TO GO. YOU'RE GOING TO GET HURT.
WHAT MORE COULD THEY DO TO ME? TO ANY OF US?

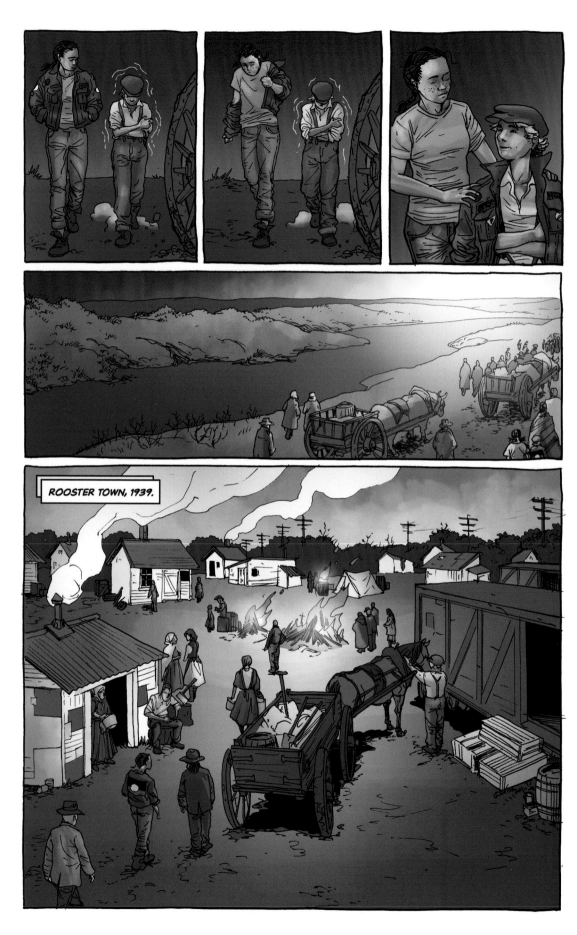

ROOSTER TOWN, 1939.

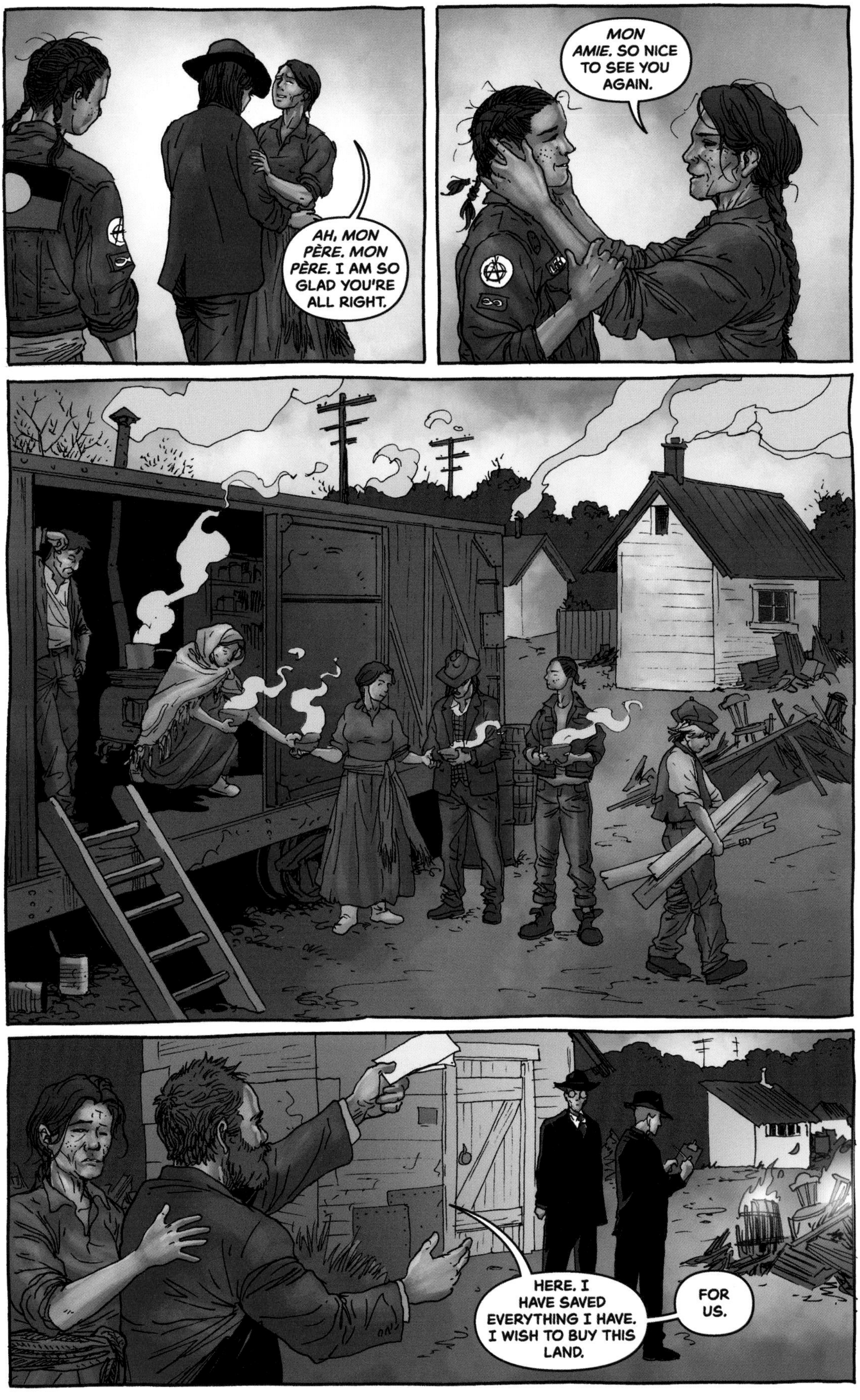
AH, MON PÈRE. MON PÈRE. I AM SO GLAD YOU'RE ALL RIGHT.
MON AMIE. SO NICE TO SEE YOU AGAIN.
HERE. I HAVE SAVED EVERYTHING I HAVE. I WISH TO BUY THIS LAND.
FOR US.

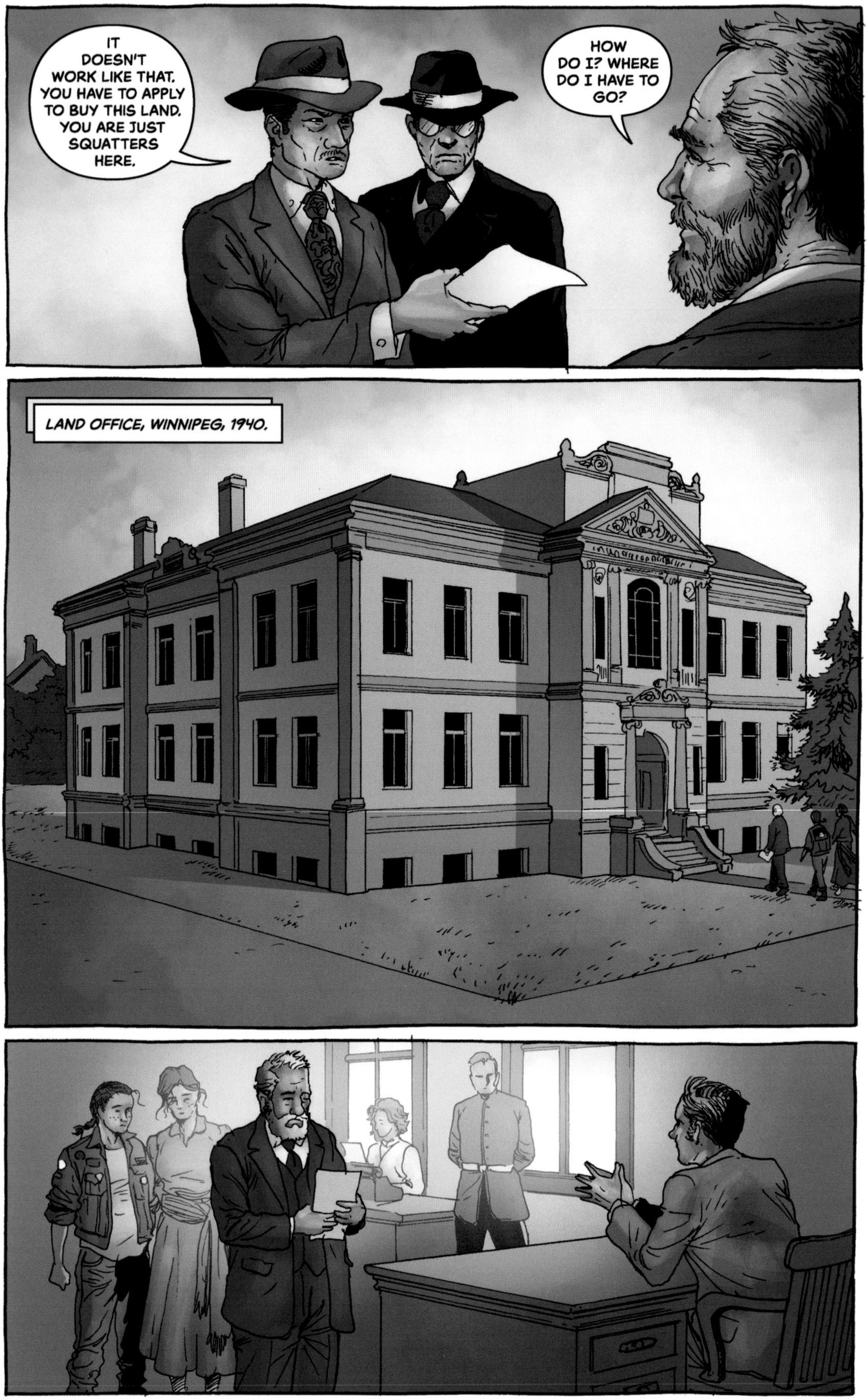
IT DOESN'T WORK LIKE THAT. YOU HAVE TO APPLY TO BUY THIS LAND. YOU ARE JUST SQUATTERS HERE.
HOW DO I? WHERE DO I HAVE TO GO?
LAND OFFICE, WINNIPEG, 1940.

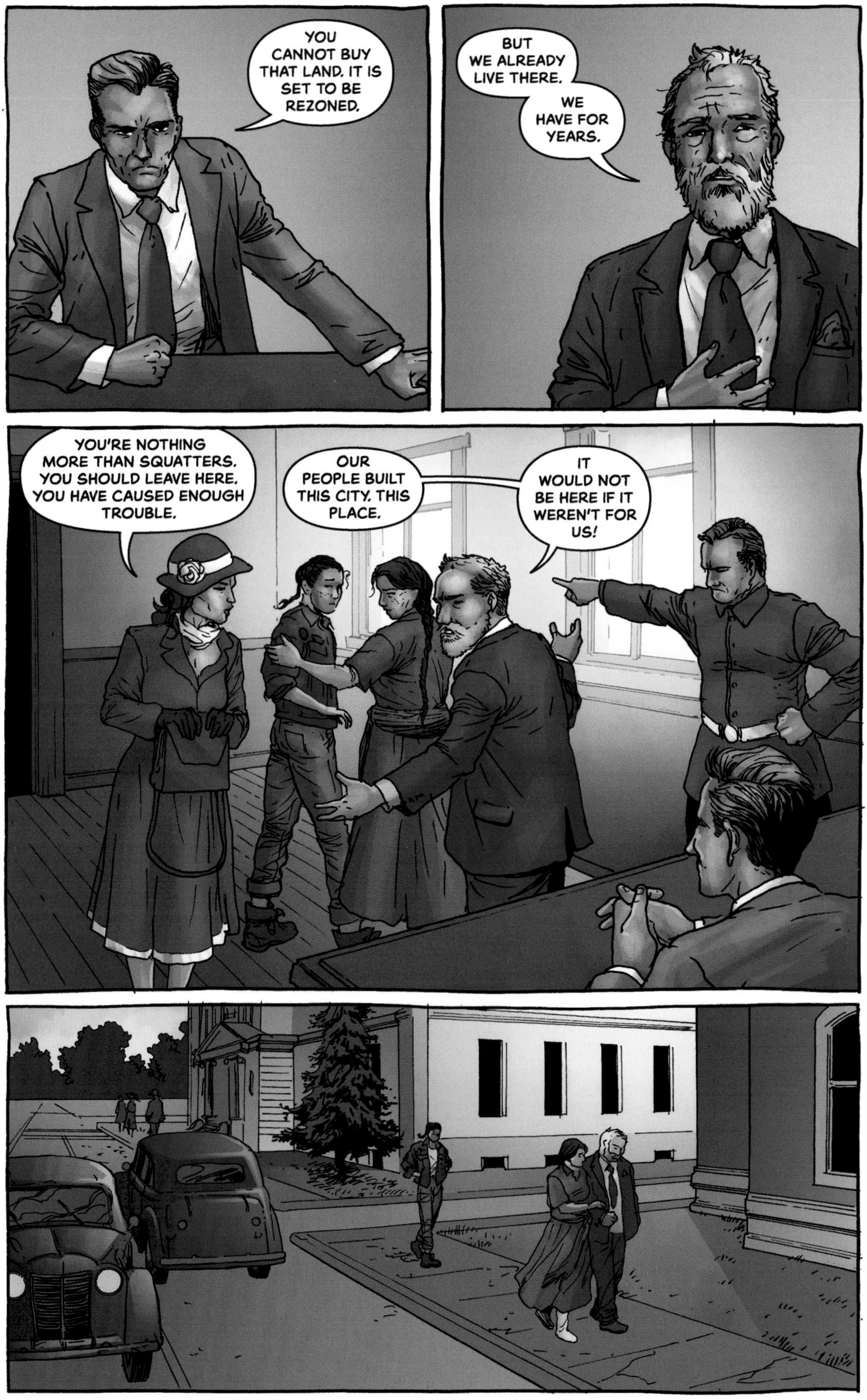
YOU CANNOT BUY THAT LAND. IT IS SET TO BE REZONED.
BUT WE ALREADY LIVE THERE.
WE HAVE FOR YEARS.
YOU'RE NOTHING MORE THAN SQUATTERS. YOU SHOULD LEAVE HERE. YOU HAVE CAUSED ENOUGH TROUBLE.
OUR PEOPLE BUILT THIS CITY. THIS PLACE.
IT WOULD NOT BE HERE IF IT WEREN'T FOR US!

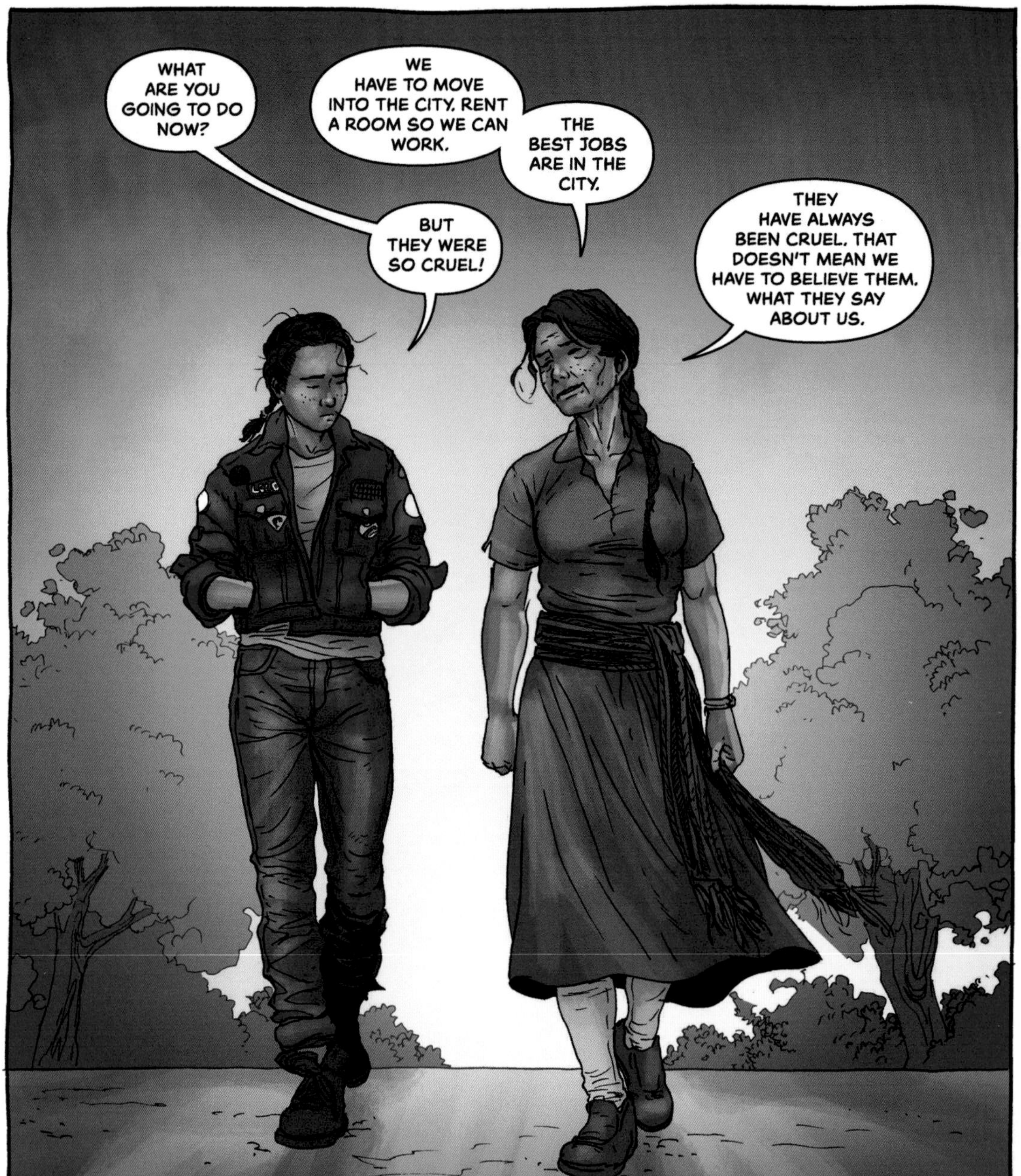
WHAT ARE YOU GOING TO DO NOW?
WE HAVE TO MOVE INTO THE CITY, RENT A ROOM SO WE CAN WORK.
THE BEST JOBS ARE IN THE CITY.
BUT THEY WERE SO CRUEL!
THEY HAVE ALWAYS BEEN CRUEL. THAT DOESN'T MEAN WE HAVE TO BELIEVE THEM. WHAT THEY SAY ABOUT US.

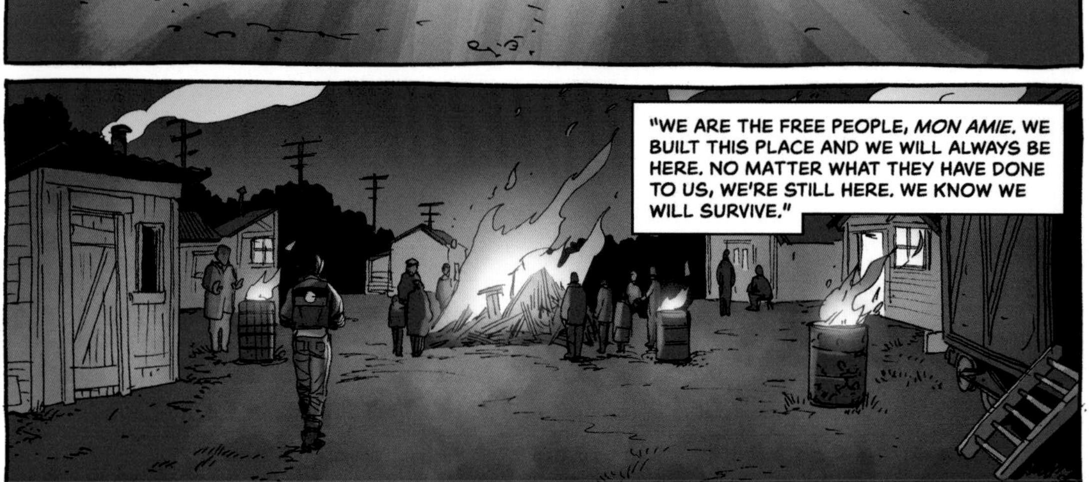
"WE ARE THE FREE PEOPLE, *MON AMIE*. WE BUILT THIS PLACE AND WE WILL ALWAYS BE HERE. NO MATTER WHAT THEY HAVE DONE TO US, WE'RE STILL HERE. WE KNOW WE WILL SURVIVE."

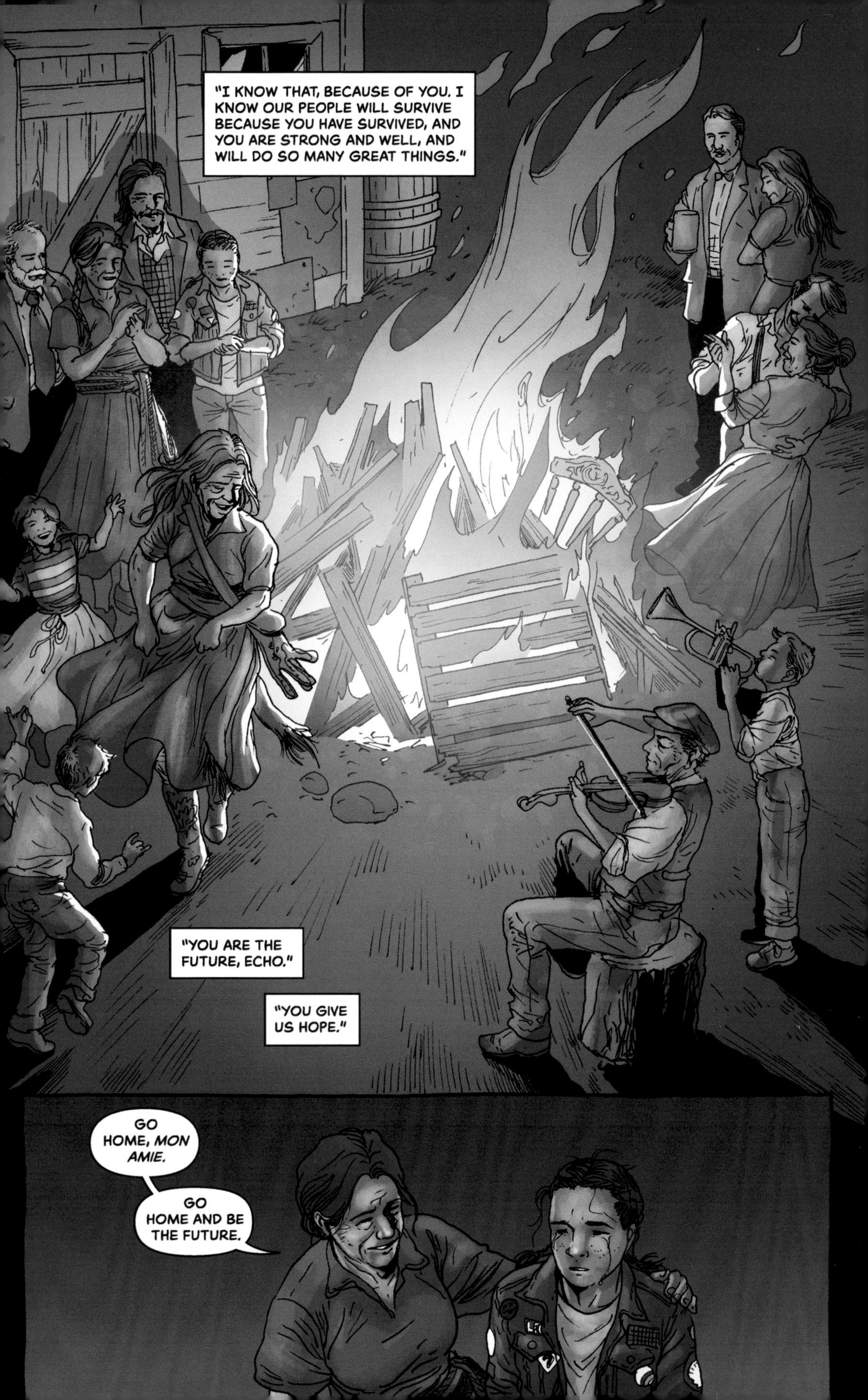
"I KNOW THAT, BECAUSE OF YOU. I KNOW OUR PEOPLE WILL SURVIVE BECAUSE YOU HAVE SURVIVED, AND YOU ARE STRONG AND WELL, AND WILL DO SO MANY GREAT THINGS."
"YOU ARE THE FUTURE, ECHO."
"YOU GIVE US HOPE."
GO HOME, *MON AMIE.*
GO HOME AND BE THE FUTURE.

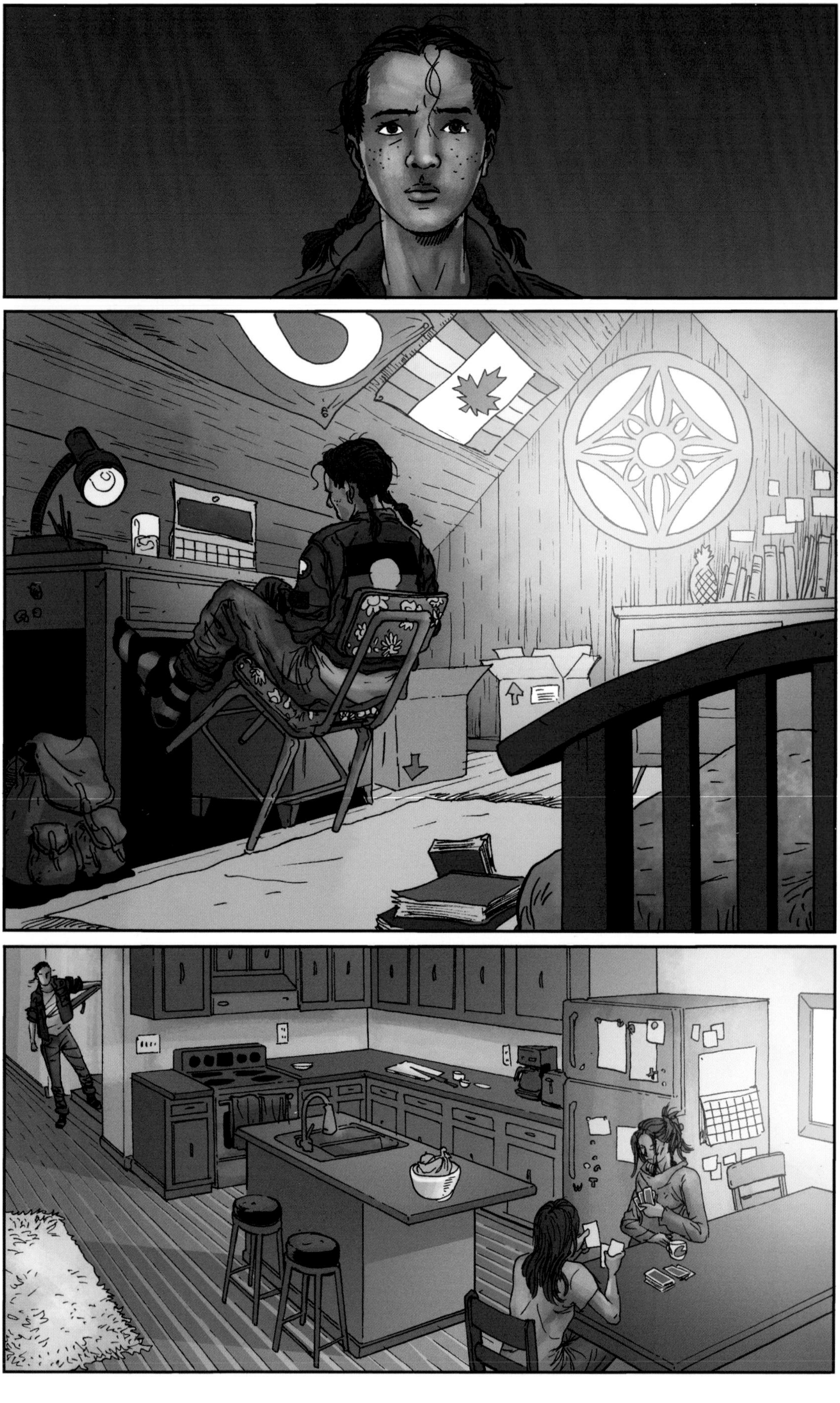

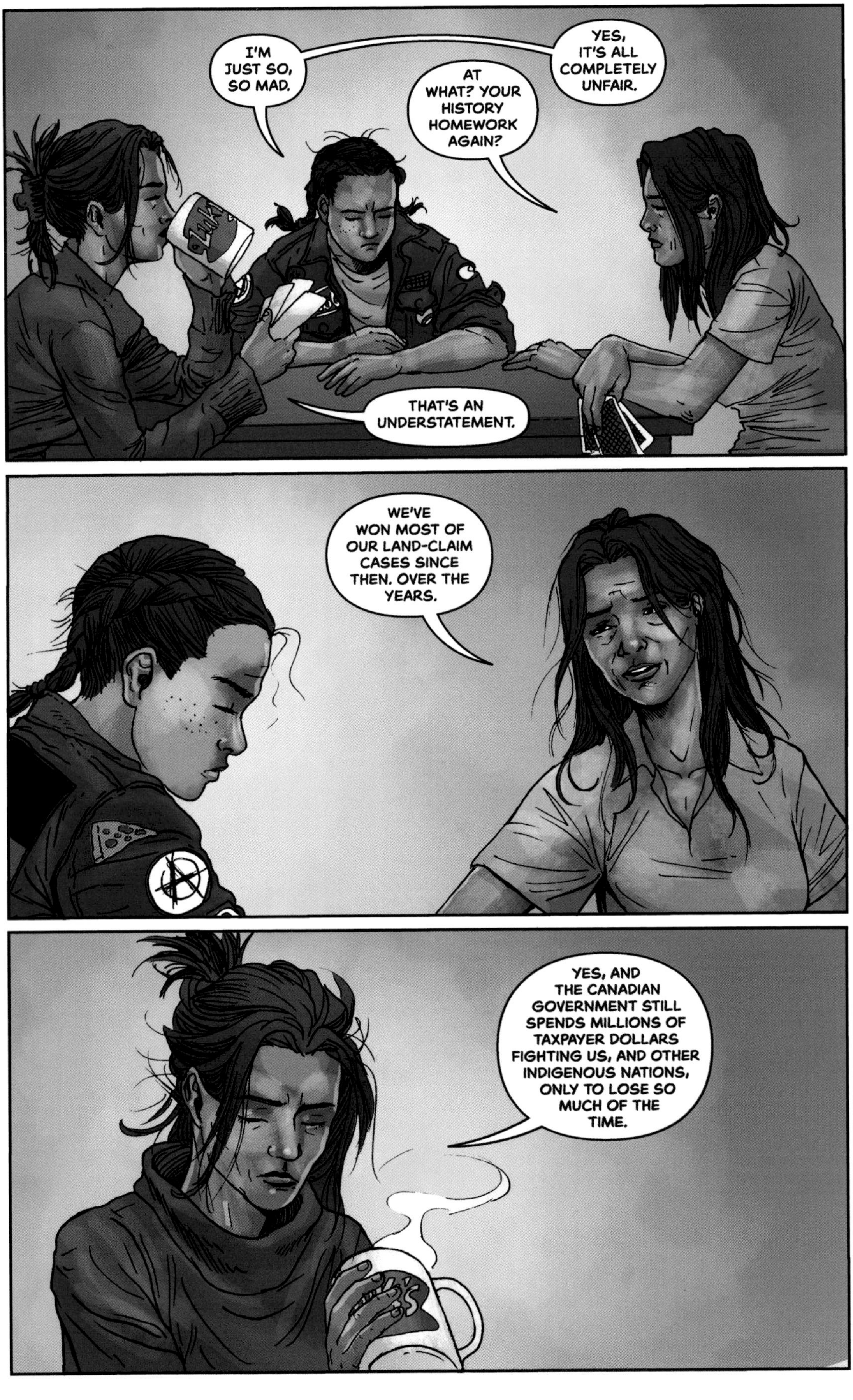
I'M JUST SO, SO MAD.
AT WHAT? YOUR HISTORY HOMEWORK AGAIN?
YES, IT'S ALL COMPLETELY UNFAIR.
THAT'S AN UNDERSTATEMENT.
WE'VE WON MOST OF OUR LAND-CLAIM CASES SINCE THEN. OVER THE YEARS.
YES, AND THE CANADIAN GOVERNMENT STILL SPENDS MILLIONS OF TAXPAYER DOLLARS FIGHTING US, AND OTHER INDIGENOUS NATIONS, ONLY TO LOSE SO MUCH OF THE TIME.

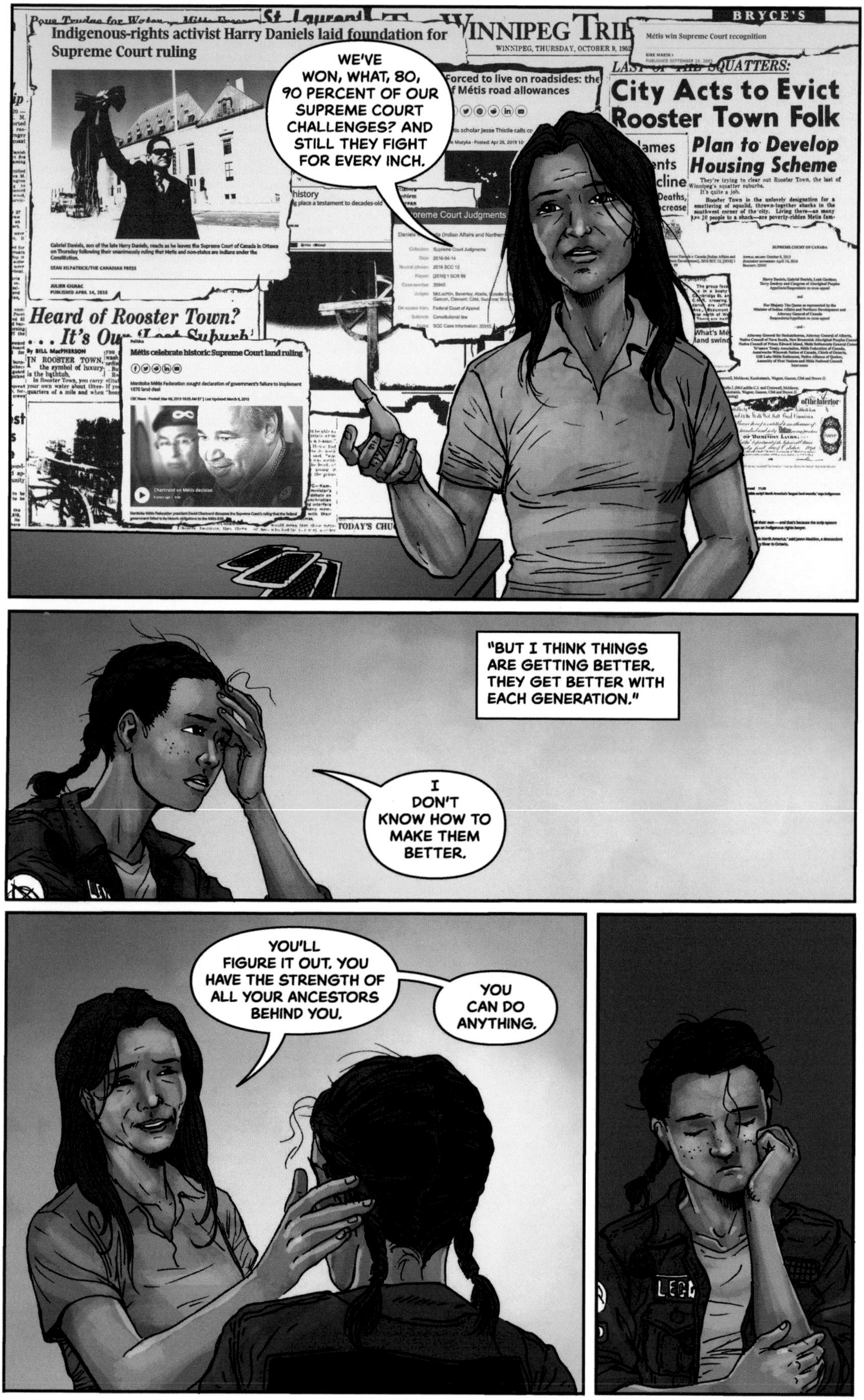
Indigenous-rights activist Harry Daniels laid foundation for Supreme Court ruling
Métis win Supreme Court recognition
City Acts to Evict Rooster Town Folk
Plan to Develop Housing Scheme
Heard of Rooster Town?
Métis celebrate historic Supreme Court land ruling
WE'VE WON, WHAT, 80, 90 PERCENT OF OUR SUPREME COURT CHALLENGES? AND STILL THEY FIGHT FOR EVERY INCH.
"BUT I THINK THINGS ARE GETTING BETTER. THEY GET BETTER WITH EACH GENERATION."
I DON'T KNOW HOW TO MAKE THEM BETTER.
YOU'LL FIGURE IT OUT. YOU HAVE THE STRENGTH OF ALL YOUR ANCESTORS BEHIND YOU.
YOU CAN DO ANYTHING.

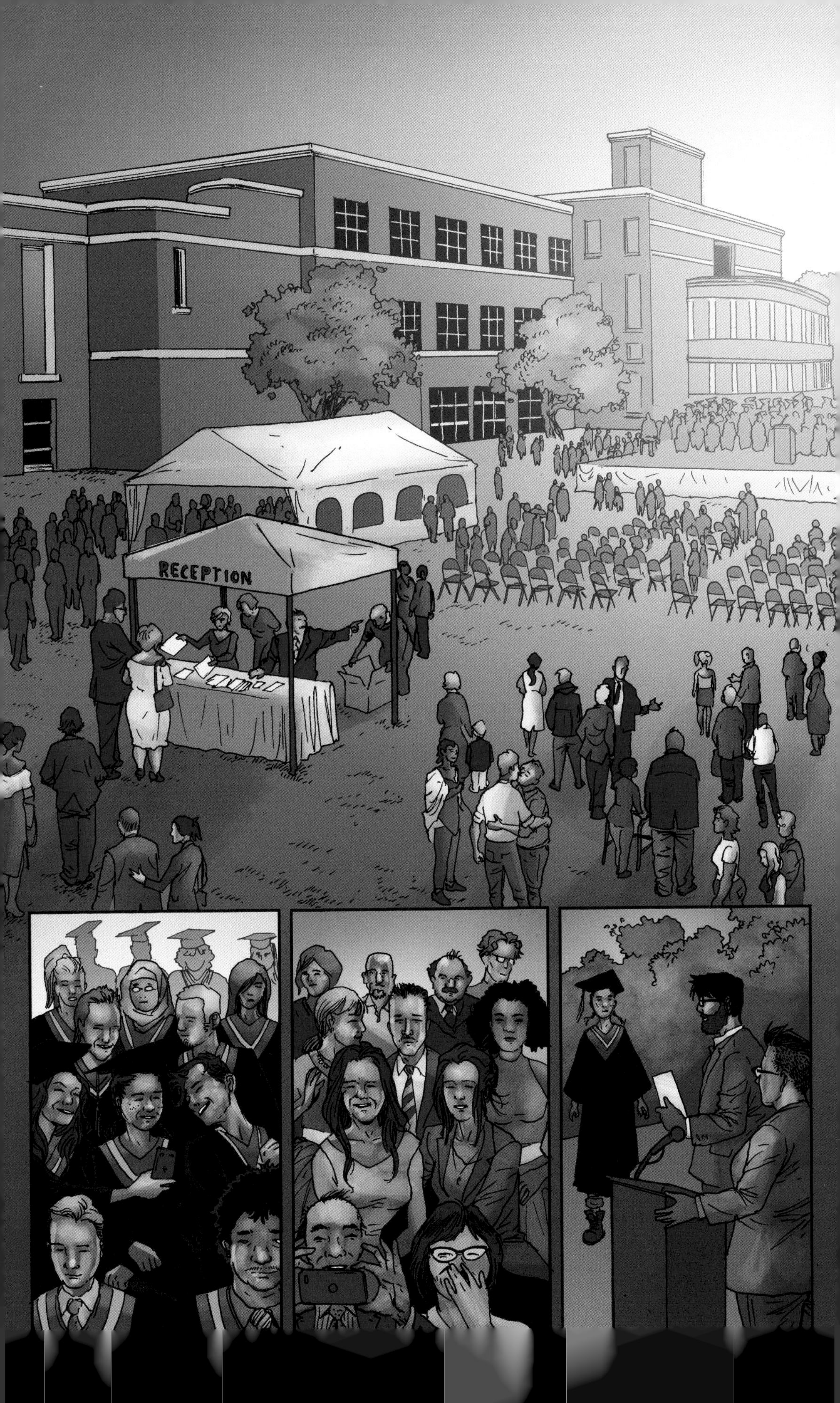
RECEPTION

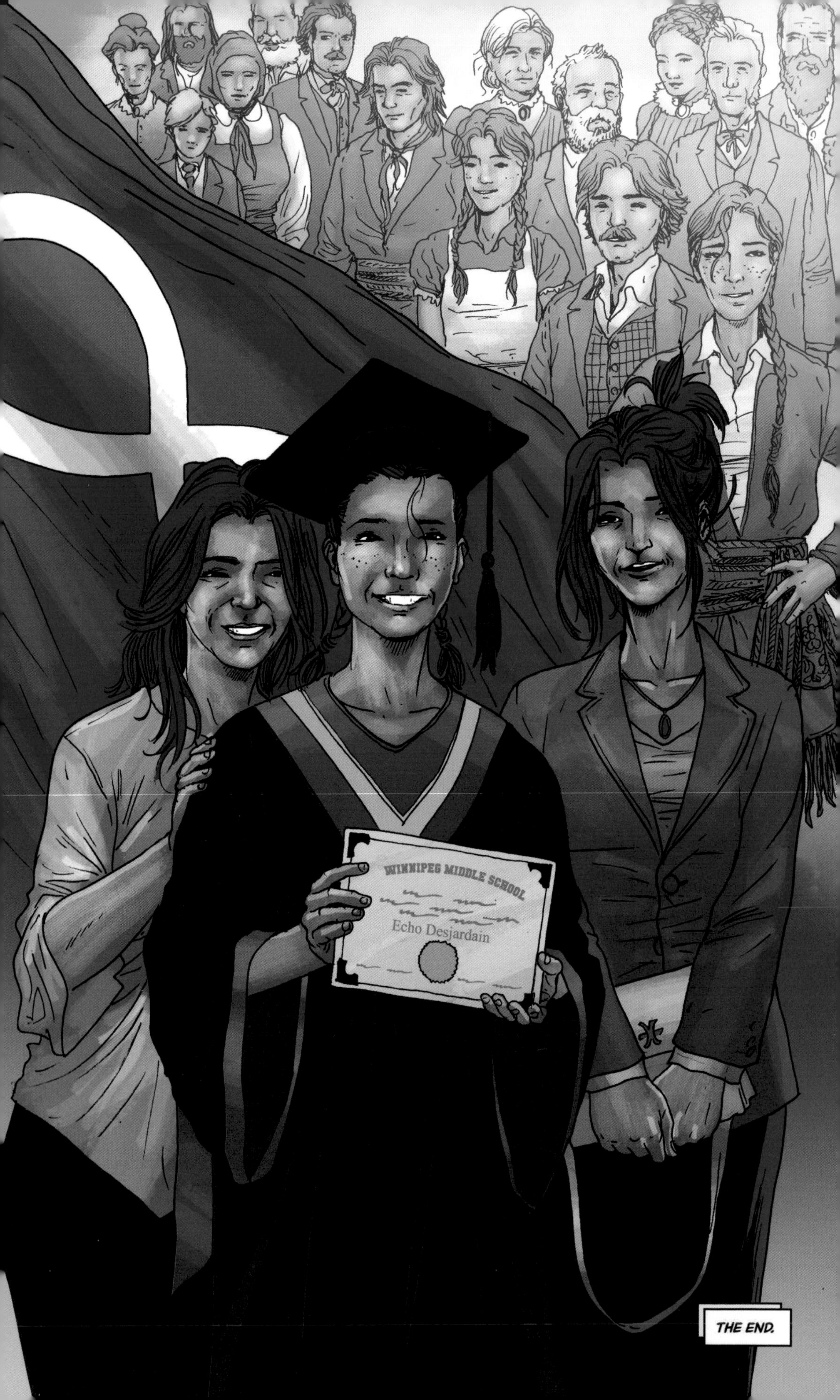
WINNIPEG MIDDLE SCHOOL
Echo Desjardain
THE END.

TIMELINE OF THE
ROAD ALLOWANCE ERA

1870

The Manitoba Act is passed, establishing the new province, and granting 1.4 million acres of land to the Métis, as well as title to the land already farmed (approximately 2.5 million acres in all).[1]

1871

The Constitution Act gives the federal Parliament power to establish new provinces.[2] Following the two-year reign of terror conducted by the Canadian Expeditionary Force against the Métis of Red River, many disperse to the West.

1872

April 14 – Dominion Lands Act is passed, providing land grants to individuals, colonization companies, and religious groups to promote settlement of the West. Claims to Métis lands and First Nations reserves, though separate from these lands, continue to be delayed.[3]

1874–1875

Legislative amendments require those applying for land to prove "undisturbed occupancy," with the result that many Métis lose their land patents as well as the right of appeal.[4]

1875

After five years' delay, the Liberal government of Alexander Mackenzie appoints representatives to verify land grant claimants. They underestimate the number of Métis children (entitled to land at age 21) at almost 2000 fewer than the 1870 census.[5]

Between 1873 and 1884, various amendments are passed that work against the Métis, and in favour of new settlers and unscrupulous land speculators. This new legislation, combined with delays in claims and encroaching poverty, force more Métis to become dispossessed and to leave their traditional homelands.[6][7]

1883

More than 70 percent of the Métis see the land they occupied in 1870 patented to others.[8]

1885

After making adjustments to the allotment, there are still 993 Métis children for whom there is no land. Instead, they each receive $240 in scrip, redeemable for land.[9]

Following the Northwest Resistance, Louis Riel is executed. The Métis lose their most ardent advocate. Branded as rebels and traitors, and with their hopes for obtaining land dashed, the Métis start to settle on road allowances and railway land, often on the fringes of urban centres. Others purchase homesteads through the Dominion Lands Act.[10]

In the late 1880s, frustrated by delays in obtaining their land grants and unnerved by the soldiers of the Canadian Expeditionary Force, some Métis families obtain homestead lands. One homestead community is Ste. Madeleine, located on the Assiniboine River in Western Manitoba, near the Saskatchewan border.

1 Ens, Gerhard. "Métis Lands in Manitoba." *Manitoba History*, no. 5, Spring 1983.
2 Ibid.
3 Yarhi, Eli, & T.D. Regehr. "Dominion Lands Act." *Canadian Encyclopedia, last updated* June 12, 2017; see also Mailhot & Sprague, "Persistent Settlers," below.
4 Mailhot, P.R., & D.N Sprague. "Persistent Settlers: The Dispersal and Resettlement of the Red River Métis, 1870-1885." *Canadian Ethnic Studies* 17, no. 2 (1985): pp. 1–31.
5 *Metis Land Use and Occupancy Study*. Birtle Transmission Project. Manitoba Metis Federation. Prepared by MNP LLP., December 2016.
6 Shore, Fred. *The Métis: Losing the Land.* Pamphlet 9. Aboriginal Information Series, August 2006.
7 Milne, Brad. "The Historiography of Métis Land Dispersal, 1870-1890." *Manitoba History*, no. 30, Autumn 1995.
8 Mailhot & Sprague, "Persistent Settlers."
9 *Metis Land Use and Occupancy Study*.
10 Shore, pamphlet 10

1901

Fifteen Métis families move to public land in the southwest corner of Winnipeg, joining six others. Originally from the St. Norbert municipality south of the city, they come seeking work. Their settlement becomes known as Rooster Town. It was also called Pakan Town (Cree for "hazelnut," a nut that grew abundantly in the area).[11]

1935

The Government of Canada, in response to severe drought from the Great Depression, enacts the Prairie Farm Rehabilitation Act to set up large community pastures for cattle grazing and conservation.

1937

The land on which Ste. Madeleine sits is claimed for community pasture. The inhabitants are informed they must vacate their land. Those who own their land but who were behind on their property taxes, as many were due to the Great Depression, are offered no compensation or alternative land.[12]

1938

The Government of Alberta passes the Métis Population Betterment Act, which creates 12 Métis colonies to address Métis inequities through farming, education, and other initiatives.[13]

1939

Ste. Madeleine is burned to the ground, its remaining citizens forced to relocate. Many move to the road allowance communities of Selby Town and The Corner, near Binscarth, Manitoba.[14]

1946

Rooster Town reaches its maximum size of 59 households, with more than 250 residents. However, within the next five years, pressure from the city's social welfare department and encroaching development compels more and more residents to leave.

1959

The remaining Rooster Town residents are evicted, given compensation of $75 per family. The homes are bulldozed and burned, and residents disperse to different city communities.[15][16]

2003

After being charged by conservation officers for hunting without a licence, Steve and Roddy Powley challenge the ruling on the basis of Indigenous hunting rights. The Supreme Court of Canada rules in their favour, and lay out the criteria, known as the Powley Test, on who qualified for such rights.

2013

The Daniels case rules that the Métis are recognized under section 91(24) of the Canadian Constitution and have a right to be consulted and negotiate with the government as Indigenous people.

11 Peters, Evelyn. "Rooster Town." *Canadian Encyclopedia*, last updated April 4, 2017.
12 *Metis Land Use and Occupancy Study*; Barkwell, Lawrence. "20th Century Métis Displacement and Road Allowance Communities in Manitoba." Winnipeg: Louis Riel Institute. November 8, 2016.
13 *Indigenous Peoples Atlas of Canada: Métis.* Ottawa: Royal Canadian Geographical Society, 2018.
14 Ibid.
15 Peters, "Rooster Town."
16 Burley, David G. "Rooster Town: Winnipeg's Lost Métis Suburb, 1900–1960." *Urban History Review* 42, no. 1 (Fall 2013): pp. 3–25.

SCRIP

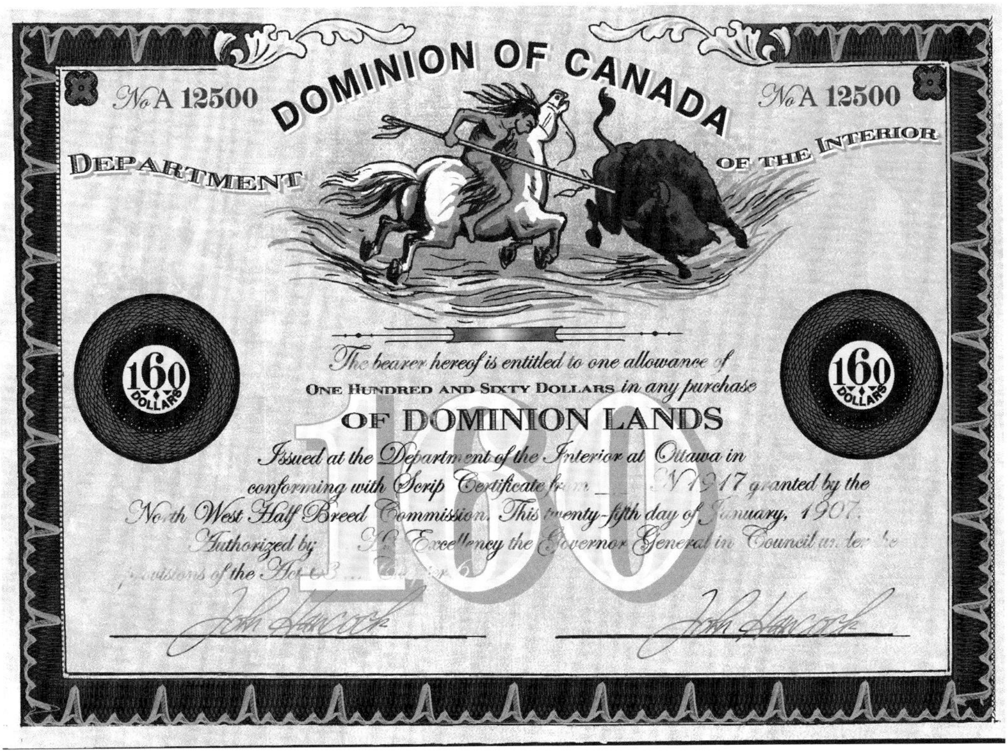
No A 12500
DOMINION OF CANADA
No A 12500
DEPARTMENT
OF THE INTERIOR
160 DOLLARS
The bearer hereof is entitled to one allowance of
One Hundred and Sixty Dollars in any purchase
of Dominion Lands
160 DOLLARS
160
Issued at the Department of the Interior at Ottawa in
conforming with Scrip Certificate
N 1917 granted by the
North West Half Breed Commission. This twenty-fifth day of January, 1907.
Authorized by
Excellency the Governor General in Council
John Hancock
John Hancock

PROOF OF SCRIP

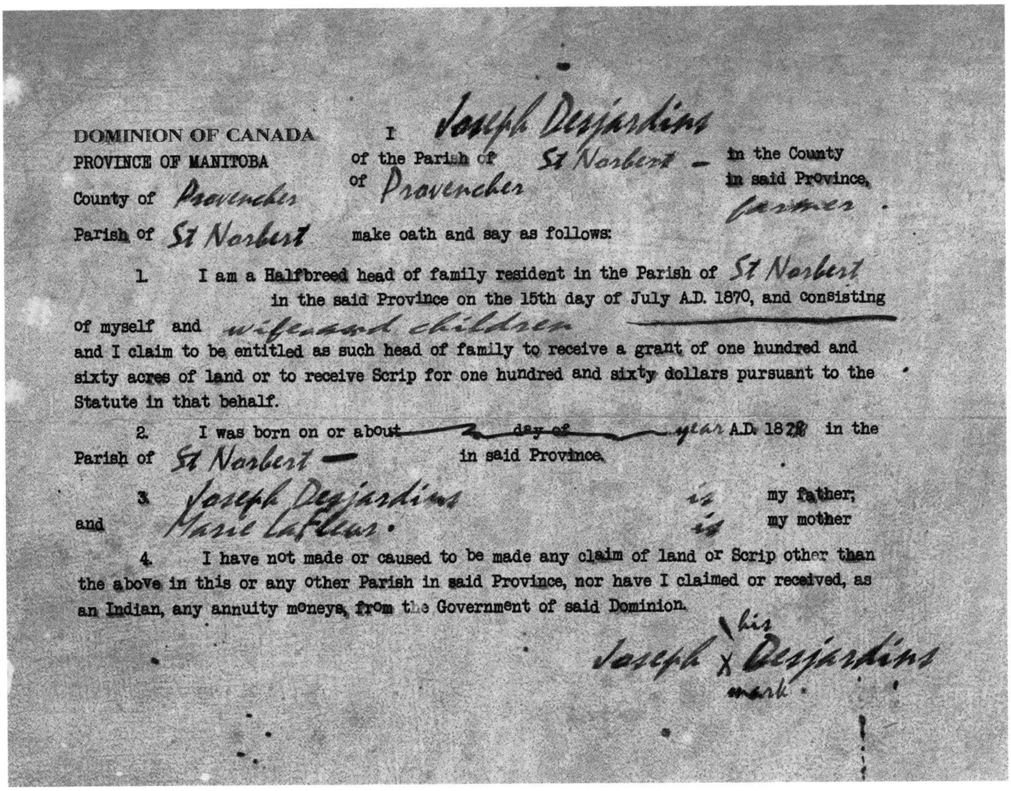

DOMINION OF CANADA
PROVINCE OF MANITOBA
County of *Provencher*
Parish of *St Norbert*

I *Joseph Desjardins* of the Parish of *St Norbert* — in the County of *Provencher* in said Province, *farmer*. make oath and say as follows:

1. I am a Halfbreed head of family resident in the Parish of *St Norbert* in the said Province on the 15th day of July A.D. 1870, and consisting of myself and *wife and children* and I claim to be entitled as such head of family to receive a grant of one hundred and sixty acres of land or to receive Scrip for one hundred and sixty dollars pursuant to the Statute in that behalf.

2. I was born on or about ~~day of~~ ~~year~~ A.D. 1828 in the Parish of *St Norbert* — in said Province.

3. *Joseph Desjardins* *is* my father; and *Marie Lafleur.* *is* my mother

4. I have not made or caused to be made any claim of land or Scrip other than the above in this or any other Parish in said Province, nor have I claimed or received, as an Indian, any annuity moneys, from the Government of said Dominion.

Joseph his X mark *Desjardins*

HighWater Press gratefully acknowledges the financial support of the Province of Manitoba through the Department of Sport, Culture and Heritage and the Manitoba Book Publishing Tax Credit, and the Government of Canada through the Canada Book Fund (CBF) for our publishing activities.

Canada Council   Conseil des Arts
for the Arts   du Canada

We also acknowledge the support of the Canada Council for the Arts.
Nous remercions le Conseil des arts du Canada de son soutien.

HighWater Press is an imprint of Portage & Main Press.
Printed and bound in Canada by Friesens
Design by Relish New Brand Experience

Library and Archives Canada Cataloguing in Publication

Title: A girl called Echo. Vol. 4, Road allowance era / by Katherena Vermette ; illustrated by
  Scott B. Henderson ; coloured by Donovan Yaciuk.

Other titles: Road allowance era

Names: Vermette, Katherena, 1977– author. | Henderson, Scott B., illustrator. | Yaciuk, Donovan,
  1975– colourist.

Identifiers: Canadiana (print) 20200302175 | Canadiana (ebook) 20200302191 | ISBN 9781553799306
  (softcover) | ISBN 9781553799313 (EPUB) | ISBN 9781553799320 (PDF)

Subjects: LCSH: Métis—History—Comic books, strips, etc. | LCSH: Métis—History—Juvenile fiction. |
  LCGFT: Graphic novels.

Classification: LCC PN6733.V47 G57 2021 | DDC j741.5/971—dc23

24 23 22 21   1 2 3 4 5

HIGHWATER
PRESS

www.highwaterpress.com
Winnipeg, Manitoba
Treaty 1 Territory and homeland of the Métis Nation